PRAISE FOR

ELIZABETH BERG AND *TAPESTRY OF FORTUNES*

"A read that's sure to make you reflect on the path your own life has taken."
—*The Huffington Post*

"This is an author who writes how women really think. . . . We've instantly promoted [*Tapestry of Fortunes*] to the top of our nightstand stack."
—*PureWow Chicago*

"[Berg] has long captivated me with her writing and, I'm happy to report, she did it again with [*Tapestry of Fortunes*]."
—*She Reads*

"Berg's writing is to literature what Chopin's études are to music—measured, delicate, and impossible to walk away from until their completion. [Grade:] A+."
—*Entertainment Weekly*

"Berg could be creating a new genre. [She] is especially wonderful at depicting the small revealing moments of women's friendships, the offhand sharing of secrets in the grocery store."
—*Kirkus Reviews*

"Elizabeth Berg's gift as a storyteller lies most powerfully in her ability to find the extraordinary in the ordinary, the remarkable in the everyday."
—*The Boston Globe*

"One of the most life-affirming writers around."
—*The Miami Herald*

"Berg has a gift for capturing the small, often sweet details of ordinary life."
—*Newsday*

TAPESTRY OF FORTUNES

TAPESTRY OF FORTUNES

A Novel

ELIZABETH BERG

BALLANTINE BOOKS
TRADE PAPERBACKS
New York

2014 Ballantine Books Trade Paperback Edition

Copyright © 2013 by Elizabeth Berg
Reading group guide copyright © 2014 by Random House LLC

Published in the United States by Ballantine Books,
an imprint of Random House, a division of Random House LLC,
a Penguin Random House Company, New York.

BALLANTINE and the HOUSE colophon are registered
trademarks of Random House LLC.
RANDOM HOUSE READER'S CIRCLE & Design is a
registered trademark of Random House LLC.

Originally published in hardcover in the United States by
Random House, an imprint of Random House,
a division of Random House LLC, in 2013.

Grateful acknowledgment is made to The Permissions Company on
behalf of Copper Canyon Press for permission to reprint an excerpt from
"Gate C22" from *The Human Line* by Ellen Bass, copyright © 2007 by
Ellen Bass. Reprinted by permission of The Permissions Company on
behalf of Copper Canyon Press, www.coppercanyonpress.org.

LIBRARY OF CONGRESS CATALOGING-IN-PUBLICATION DATA
Berg, Elizabeth.
Tapestry of fortunes: a novel / Elizabeth Berg.
p. cm.
ISBN 978-0-345-53379-1
eBook ISBN 978-0-679-64469-9
1. Female friendship—Fiction.   I. Title.
PS3552.E6996T37 2013
813'.54—dc23   2012033033

Printed in the United States of America on acid-free paper

www.randomhousereaderscircle.com

4 6 8 9 7 5 3

Book design by Barbara M. Bachman

The gift of how to read the omens and hear my fellow creatures, to see the place where future lives and sing Great Mystery's songs is what I want to share. It comes from my heart and it is good.

—*Jamie Sams, Hancoka Olowanpi*

TAPESTRY OF FORTUNES

When I was growing up, my mother's best friend was a woman named Cosmina Mandruleanu. I liked her for a lot of reasons: her name, of course; her ash-blond hair and throaty voice and loud laugh; her bangle bracelets and black nylons and the way she was generous with the Juicy Fruit gum she always kept in her purse. She was someone who made smoking seem alluring; if she looked at you in that sidelong way when she exhaled, you felt as though you were sharing a risqué secret. She told me her grandmother was a Romanian gypsy who had passed on to her the Gift: Cosmina could tell fortunes. Mostly she used tea leaves, but she also read palms or used a crystal ball or her grandmother's ancient Tarot cards. She said her gifts were in her mind, that she could use anything, even a pair of pliers, as a catalyst for accessing her powers. But people liked the traditional props, and so she accommodated them. She once told my mother that she, too, was a bit psychic, which made my mother fluff up with pride and say, "You know, I thought so." When I asked Cosmina if she thought I had the Gift as well, she looked at me for a long time. Then she said, "You are a good student of human nature. That's a start."

Cosmina once volunteered to tell fortunes at my junior high school's annual fund-raiser, so that the adults would have something to do besides drink weak coffee and watch Dunk the Principal. She sat in a corner of the gymnasium behind a TV tray on which she had draped a black cloth, and she wore a long black skirt and a black blouse over which she had a fringed red shawl. She'd knotted a black scarf at the base of her neck to cover her bright hair, and her makeup was more dramatic than usual: thick lines of kohl were drawn around her eyes. I offered her a dollar to have my own fortune read. She refused at first; she said she read adults only, it wasn't right to read children, especially children of your friends. Finally, though, she relented. I stood before her in my pedal pushers and sleeveless blouse, my breath caught in my throat. She laid her hands on her crystal ball and closed her eyes. Then she peered into it. After a moment, she said, "Your task will be to learn in what direction to look for life's great riches, and not to deny the veracity of your own vision."

I stared at her, then whispered, "What does 'veracity' mean?"

She leaned forward and whispered back, "Truth."

When I got outside, I wrote Cosmina's words on the back of a flyer. That night, I read them again, then put the paper in a handmade wooden box I'd been given by my grandfather. It was large, about twelve by twenty, and four inches deep, made of black ash; and it had box-joint corners of which the maker was justifiably proud. He'd woodburned Japanese chrysanthemums into the lid, and they were beautiful—spidery and reaching, botanical fireworks. I'd wanted to save the box to use for something important. Here it was.

My best friend Penny's grave has a simple headstone, light gray granite inscribed with her name, the date of her birth, and the date of her death, which was four months ago. Below that, as agreed, are these words: *Say it.* Penny believed that people didn't often enough admit to what they really felt, and she thought that made for a lot of problems. Being close to her meant that you had to attempt unstinting honesty, at least in your dealings with her. Her husband, Brice, could get annoyed about this, and so could I—a lack of deceit requires a kind of internal surveillance that can feel like work, and there are, after all, times when a lie serves a noble purpose. But overall, I think both he and I understood the value of such candor, and appreciated Penny's efforts to steer us toward it. And then there was this: we wanted to please her because we both loved her so much. Loved and needed her.

And here she is.

I lean back on my hands and look out over the acres of graves. I used to feel that cemeteries were wasted space, that they could be put to far better use as parks, or golf courses, or even to allow for more living space. But I've changed my mind. There is a wide peace here, even in sorrow; and it's sitting beside Penny's grave that I can best feel her.

"Going to Atlanta tomorrow," I tell her.

Good gig?

"It is good. Early flight, though. You know I hate those early flights."

Stop whining.

"Your sweet peas are blossoming," I say. I planted some recently, at the base of her headstone.

I know. I see. Pink.

"Where are you?"

Silence.

"Penny?"

She's gone.

She always leaves when I ask that question; I don't know why I keep asking it. Well, yes I do. I keep asking it because I keep wanting to know where she is.

I sit for a while longer, appreciating the feel of the sun on my back, the sound of the mockingbird in the tree nearby imitating the whistle of a cardinal. A few rows away, I see an old man sitting on a fold-up chair, his hat in his hands, his head bowed. I can see his lips moving. It might be prayer. Or he might be like me: he might be having a conversation. Out here, there are a lot of people like me. We don't often speak to each other, but I think it's safe to say we gratefully acknowledge each other's presence, that little mercy.

THE NEXT AFTERNOON, I'M AT THE OSHAKA WOMEN'S CLUB IN Atlanta, where I've been hired to give a talk. I'm standing at the window in the speaker's room and looking through the slanted blinds at the women gathered on the lawn, chatting amiably, laughing, leaning their heads together to share a certain confidence. They're pretty; they look like so many butter mints, dressed in pastel greens and pinks and yellows and whites. It's a warm spring day after a rainy night, and the women who are wearing high heels are having trouble with them sinking into the earth.

I sit down on the silk love seat to review my notes, but I don't have to: I've delivered this speech called "You.2: Creating a Better Version of Yourself" so many times, in so many places, that I've pretty much memorized it. But looking at my notes gives me something to do besides stare at the flowered wallpaper, the Oriental rug, the gold-and-crystal sconce lighting, which I've already examined thoroughly. It also keeps me from what has become a persistent sadness; it's taking me a while to get over Penny's death. The last thing a motivational speaker needs is to appear low on energy, mired in despair.

This organization likes you to be there early, and they keep you in the speaker's room until you go on; they feel it's more exciting to their audience if they see you for the first time when you come onstage, smiling, waving, dressed in your power suit—in this case, a white St. John skirt and jacket, offset by a turquoise necklace and earrings.

A fifty-something woman wearing a yellow apron over a print dress comes into the room holding a little gold-rimmed plate full of food: tea sandwiches, cut-up melon, cookies. "I'm just helping out in the kitchen before your talk," she says. "I have to tell you, I am really looking forward to hearing you speak. I hope you won't mind my telling you this, but you said something in your last book that truly helped change my life: *Getting lost is the only way to find what you didn't know you were looking for.* It is so true. It helped me to flat out leave a man who was just a son of a bitch, plain and simple. It took a real leap of faith to do what you said. I *did* have to get kind of lost—to abandon certain ways of thinking, of *being*, really—and it was scary. But doing that gave me the courage to walk away from someone I should have left a long time ago. And six months later, I found someone else who is much better for me. I'm so happy to thank you in person for helping me to do that."

She looks at her watch, unties her apron. "Oh my, I didn't mean to run on. I'd better get a seat."

She goes out of the room and I check my makeup one more time, straighten my suit jacket, and here comes Darlene Simmons, the club's president, to escort me onto the stage.

When we come out from behind the curtain, the room immediately quiets. I sit in one of the two wingback chairs onstage, and Darlene goes up to the lectern and does the introduction. Then I go up and begin my talk.

Forty minutes later, I end by saying, "When I was a junior in high school, I was sitting in my world history class when the teacher suddenly asked this question: 'What is truth?' There was a long silence, we all just sat there, and then finally Janet Gilmore, the smartest girl in the class—and also, unfairly, the prettiest—raised her hand and she said, 'Truth is what you believe.' Mr. Sanders nodded approvingly. I was thinking, *What does this have to do with history?* But of course it has everything to do with history, because history is shaped by the belief systems of those who made it.

"Our own individual life history is also shaped that way. In large part, when you factor out fate, what we are is because of what we believe about ourselves. Wherever we are in the world, we mostly live in the small space between our ears.

"I challenge you to acknowledge and affirm your innermost beliefs: bring them into the light. When you know what the truth is for you, you can help create not only your history, but your destiny."

I thank the audience, then step from behind the lectern to applaud them. I've been doing this long enough to know that many women are inspired, but some who walked in here cynical are walking out the same way. In some respects, I'm among them. But if there's one thing I've learned in my years as a motivational speaker, it's that most people need someone else to tell them what they already know. I include myself in this. I include myself most keenly. That, in fact, is how I start my talks: I say I am forever a physician in the act of healing myself, that to be human is to live in wonder and in need, and in perpetual evolution. I say that no matter what our occupation, our real job is to help each other out. Penny was the one who helped me. It kills me to use the past tense when I talk about her. It frightens me to think that there may never be anyone who can take her place.

Times when we were stumped and unable to advise each other about problems, we used to go out on my porch at night with my grandfather's box. We would light candles and hunch over a table and inquire of the oracle. In addition to Cosmina's fortune, which I wrote

out all those years ago, the box holds a lot of different things for playing medium: cards, books, stones.

Penny and I asked about relationships, about work, about friends
and relatives, and occasionally about politicians. We asked if the end
of the world was nigh; we asked if the Twins would win the series. We
were often playful but just as often we were deeply respectful. It was
eerie how "on" the answers sometimes were, how using two or even
three different methods for posing the same question could yield the
same answer. I think on more than one occasion we kind of scared
ourselves.

And then there was the time after Penny was first diagnosed, when
I did the cards alone. I sat at my kitchen table and closed my eyes and
simply thought, *Penny.* I was too afraid to ask a specific question. But
the question was heard anyway, because I pulled the death card. I
reshuffled the deck once, twice, and made a new spread. Pulled a
card. Got the same thing.

I laid my head down on my arms and wept. Since that day, I, the
motivational speaker, have not been able to motivate myself into making a new life without her.

"I'LL STOP SOON," I USED TO TELL PENNY, WHO IN RECENT YEARS had begun advising me to quit working or at least cut down enough so that we could travel together. It was a dream of ours to go to Japan; I think Penny bought every book published about traveling there. We also wanted to take a leisurely driving trip across the southern states. Brice didn't like to travel and was all in favor of Penny "getting it out of her system" with me. I had never married, and though I almost always had a relationship, sometimes a serious one, I never thought any of those men would be as much fun to travel with as Penny would be. We were passionate about many of the same things: small towns, vintage quilts, unique breakfast places, cobalt-blue glassware, spontaneous conversations with all kinds of people in all kinds of places. Penny was the kind of person who could go into a convenience store for a Coke and come out soul mates with the cashier.

We also seemed to operate on the same kind of schedule; it was a happy day when we admitted to each other that we loved taking the phone off the hook and napping in the mid-afternoons. "Do you sleep more than twenty minutes?" I asked. I felt a little guilty that my naps lasted thirty or even forty-five minutes. "I have gone for two *hours!*" she said, and I high-fived her.

We planned on alternating extravagant hotels with cheap motels on our road trip. "Maybe we'll find a crumbly old pink one!" Penny said. "With one of those pools the size of a puddle!" It was our belief that tacky motels would be much more interesting, even if the beds gave pause. We wanted to walk the Freedom Trail in Boston and take donkeys down into the Grand Canyon. We wanted to feel the power of the vortexes in Sedona, Arizona, and to buy some crystals there. Oh, we had plans. So many plans that I kept putting off.

"But *when* will you stop?" she would ask, year after year, and I would say, "Something will tell me when." Once, exasperated, she said, "You act like there's all the time in the world, and there isn't!" To this I had no reply.

That Penny and Brice Mueller lived right next door to me was a gift of immeasurable proportion. I used to go into their house as though it were my own. We watched television a couple of nights a week and we often made dinners and ate together. Every Sunday, we used my living room to read the papers while we ate caramel rolls from Keys Café; the three of us were almost roommates. I used to tell them that they, more than anyone else I had ever met, supported my theory that people are attracted to those who look like themselves. Brice and Penny were both very tall, with strawberry-blond hair, wide eyes, freckled arms and legs. Even the shape of their noses was similar. Where they differed was in their personalities: Penny was always up for almost anything; Brice was far more cautious. Penny was an optimist, too, sometimes outright irritating in her consistently bright outlook; Brice had his moods. But they were good together; they loved each other, and they were so much fun to be around.

When Brice's birthday was coming up, I hid his presents in my bedroom closet. I hid Penny's in the furnace room; she was in my closet too often for me to risk putting anything there. There were times when I was at their house late at night and moaned about being too tired to walk across the lawn to my own house. They would invite me to stay and I would always say that was ridiculous and rally myself to make the short trip. But I think if I'd ever said, "Oh hell, why don't I just move in?" they would have looked at each other, shrugged, and said, "Sure!"

Eight months ago, Penny was diagnosed with a fast-moving cancer; she died four months later. Brice stayed in the house for another month. Then he came over one night with a bottle of wine and told me he knew he wasn't supposed to make any rash moves, everyone had told him that, including me, but the hell with it, he was going to move back to New York. He said he couldn't stand being in the house—or the city, or the state, or the Midwest—without her. When we had finished the bottle, he said, "You know, Penny told me that when she died, I should marry you."

I smiled. "I know. She told me the same thing, that I should marry you. So what did you say, when she told you that?"

"What did you say?" Brice asked.

"Okay. Let's both answer on three. One . . . two . . . ."

On three, we both said, *"Naaaah."*

"Not that I don't love you," Brice said, quickly.

"Or I you."

"But . . ." he said.

"But," I agreed.

He got up and stood looking out onto the street for a while, his hands on his hips like a quarterback. Then he turned and said, "Well."

"Take care of yourself, B," I said, and I watched him walk back to his house—their house—his head hung low.

A moving van pulled away from that house two weeks later, and a week after that another moving van pulled up to it. A young family lives next door now, very nice, two little boys, six and eight. They're wonderful children, polite and charming and oftentimes funny, but for me the whole family is like being offered a sumptuous dinner when you've no appetite at all.

Lately, I've been thinking I need to move, too. *When?* I ask myself sometimes, and I answer in the same way I answered Penny: something will tell me when.

Well, maybe that has just happened: maybe something is telling me that now is the time. Getting off the plane on my way home from making the speech in Atlanta, I have one of those moments that feels like life backing up to you without the warning beeps, and then hitting you smack in the middle of your chest. I realize what it is: I don't want to go home. Not to that house, not to that street. The thought of pulling into the driveway, sliding the key into the lock, offers not the comfort of familiarity but the ache of abandonment.

On the plane, I sat next to a man with whom I had a great deal in common. We both liked anchovies and we were born in the same month in the same year. We liked Little League baseball, we loved dogs but traveled too much to have one. Our hair was the same salt-and-pepper color. The most salient thing we had in common was that we both had jobs motivating people. But whereas I wrote self-help books and gave talks, he was a psychologist who flew around the country to various businesses, doing team building with employees. He enjoyed his work, and he had been remarkably successful. He told me that at one time he had owned four homes, including an apartment in Paris. Now, though, he was coming back from having done his last job. He was quitting the business, and he and his wife were going to live in the one place he had left—he'd sold all the others. They were going to live in a small cabin, located on Burntside Lake in northern Minnesota, near the Boundary Waters.

"Retiring, huh?" I said.

He looked over at me. "I don't call it that. I guess I don't even think of it like that. I see where all this success has led me. Now I want to see what it's kept me from."

"Huh," I said. And then I asked him, "Are you at all scared?"

He tossed some peanuts into his mouth, leaned in closer to me, and said, "Terrified."

We both laughed, but then he said, "I also haven't felt this alive in years."

I sit in one of the empty gate areas to call a cab. When the dispatcher asks where I'm going and I give him my address, my gut begins to ache. Well, I've said it often enough to others: there are times when you have to hurt badly in order to move. Otherwise, you'll stay in a place you've outgrown.

When I get out to the curb, the cab is there. The driver stashes my bag in the trunk, and I think he looks angry. Sure enough, as we pull away from the curb, he catches my eyes in the rearview and in an accent I can't quite identify yells, "You know what? I'll tell you something: People are rude!"

"They certainly can be," I say.

"For one hour, I been waiting for a man who say he's coming right out, that's what he tell the starter, 'No, I have no baggage; I am coming out now.' *One hour* I wait, he doesn't come. Then the starter tell me, 'He went to baggage claim; he's coming now.'

"I say, 'No.' I say, 'I'm not take him.' Instead, I take you."

From the radio, I hear the faint strains of "September in the Rain."

"Is that Dinah Washington?" I ask, leaning forward.

The man, whose name is Khaled, has settled down somewhat; he readjusts his shoulders and increases the volume slightly.

"Yes, Dinah Washington, I have to listen to her because she make me calm down from the *rude people.*"

I lean back in the seat, cross my arms, and stare out the window. "I wish there was a place where you could sit at a little table and still listen to songs like that," I say. "You know. White tablecloth, little lamp lit low, Rob Roys and Brandy Alexanders."

"Those places are all gone, now."

"I know they are."

We fall silent until we pull up in front of my house. Then Khaled says, "I tell you what. You hire me and I drive you around and all we do, we listen to old songs. For many hours!"

I laugh. "Don't tempt me."

I bring my bags in, then collect the mail and start sorting through it. For one moment, I think about calling Khaled back. But I don't. I hope it is not to my everlasting regret. I'm always telling everyone else to take advantage of spontaneous gifts that come along, often when you least expect them. In fact, that idea inspired one of my books, the one that emphasizes the worth of going out into the world and gathering up all the beautiful things that are given to you, if only you will ask.

I am just about to toss all the mail in the trash when what I think is a postcard falls out of a circular. But it's not a postcard. Rather, it's an old black-and-white photograph made to serve as a postcard, of what looks to be Tahiti: there in the background is the endless sea, the rise of low mountains, wisps of clouds. In the foreground, off to the side, is a black-haired native woman with an unsettlingly direct gaze. I have never seen the image, yet it is familiar to me.

On the back of the card, I see lines of black ink from a fountain pen, written in a clear, flowing hand that I recognize instantly. The message is brief, only three lines:

> *I still think of you.*
> *How are you?*
> *Tell me.*

There is a return address, no name, but I don't need one. From both the image and the handwriting, I know who sent this photo: Dennis Halsinger. He is an artist I once loved, who left Minnesota for Tahiti many years ago. His name is such a long story.

Well. Speaking of everlasting regret.

Once I was riding a bus, sitting behind two women who were maybe in their late fifties. They were engrossed in a conversation I couldn't hear much of; they kept their voices low and decorous. But at one point, one of the women sighed and leaned her head against the bus window, and said, "Ah, you know. *My one and only yous.*"

Her friend laughed. "It's my one and only *you.*"

The other woman said, "No it isn't."

I think it's true for a lot of people, that we have a few shining relationships in our lives, with people we hold forever in our hearts. It also seems, though, that there's usually one who mattered most. For me, that was Dennis Halsinger. He was the one apart, the one I loved best, and truest, and the one I felt most loved by. I loved him for the way he was and for who I was when I was with him. He lived honestly, consciously, in ways both macro and micro, and I admired this. Morning, noon, middle of the night: when you looked into his eyes, the sign was flipped to the Open side. I could tell him anything, and did. We fit together in much the same easy way that Penny and I did. It was rare enough for me to have that ease and joy and depth in a friendship with a woman; to have the same level of comfort with a man was something I had never experienced before, nor have I since. Even in my most successful relationships after Dennis, there was only so far I could go. Or would go, perhaps.

When Dennis and I were both still in our early twenties, he left, he went off on a voyage to South America, and later to Tahiti, to live. We'd planned on my joining him there. But in the end I lacked the courage to break away like that. It had all seemed so easy when I agreed to it, but then there was the matter of getting the money for the plane ticket, of deciding what to take and what not to. Would they have Herbal Essences shampoo there? Good movies and record stores? What if I got appendicitis? Would I in fact miss the country I spent so much time maligning? In the end, I decided to pass on the idea. *For the moment!* I told myself. I believed, in youth's way, that such opportunities would always be there. Such men, too, I suppose.

Anyway, gradually, Dennis and I lost touch. And then we died, is how I now realize I thought of it. Or maybe it was just a part of me that died, when I didn't go with him.

But now. Here he is, on a card in my hand. Dennis Halsinger!

I don't even bother to change out of my suit. I go directly to the little desk in the bedroom and take out stationery. Images of Dennis from the time we were together are tumbling around in my brain, falling over themselves for prime placement: his long blond hair, his face so handsomely chiseled I used to tell him he should model for Prince Valiant in the comics. I see us walking in a field with chest-high grass that moved in the wind like water, and where the birdsong was so loud it made us laugh—we had to shout to be heard above it. I remember us driving down the freeway on a hot August night, look-ing for a place far from city lights where we could lie down and look at the stars, and the place we found presented constellations to us with a clarity that rendered us speechless.

Dennis used to give books to me, battered paperbacks he had read and reread into buttery softness: *Siddhartha, The Magic Mountain, Fear and Trembling*. He said I'd learn more from them than from my psychology textbooks, and he was right. He gave me the *I Ching*, the edition with the foreword by Carl Jung, and we did our fist toss using pennies on the sidewalk in front of his house.

In addition to photography, Dennis did painting and sculpture, and I remember him up on a ladder barefoot and shirtless, his jeans barely hanging on to his slim hips, welding something onto a high, free-form tower he had made—he did at least wear a welder's mask. I remember his hand guiding mine as he showed me how to draw a peony as big as a dinner plate. Feeding me the seeds of a pomegranate, one by one. The time we jumped in the Mississippi to go swimming and, afterward, came back to my place to dry off. We sat at the tiny kitchen table wrapped in towels and then he stood and dropped his towel and said, "This is the way I was born." I stood and my towel dropped, too, and I went to him and he carried me to my bed. That was my first time; he was the first, and I've always been glad of that.

I begin writing:

Dear Dennis,

A few months ago, I started a letter to you. But there was too much to say. It was a time when I had just lost my best friend, and I was casting about for what to do with myself, needing to remember that life is mostly rich and beautiful and ever there for the taking. And if there was anyone who could remind me of that, it was you. But I wrote a few lines, and stopped.

Then, today, I got your postcard. And your photograph,
wonderful as always.

Dennis used to take photos of ordinary people, beautiful images that you wanted to stare and stare at, that your eye roved over and kept finding things in. He took pictures in a casual, off-the-cuff kind of way, and I never understood how he was able to find the precise moment to snap the shutter. By showing a half smile, a finger to the corner of the eye, an unbandaged cut on a hand, he could reveal so much about a person. Sometimes it wasn't the people themselves; it was their houses, or their cars, or their four dogs. It was random things that belonged to them—a tin of buttons. Brass knuckles in a bedside drawer. A cookbook open to a page with so many stains it looked like a Rorschach test.

Looking at Dennis's photos showed me that photography was not only visual record keeping but a legitimate form of art. Not only did I see that a person's soul could be captured (the Native Americans were right to fear the lens), but I saw how shadow and light affect the image. And I saw what Dennis meant when he said that photography is a process of elimination.

He once showed me a collection of photographs he'd taken of waitresses when he drove his motorcycle from Minnesota to California. You could see all the different uniforms, the white shoes, the variety of earrings, one lovely locket on a long chain. I remember a shot where a waitress had six plates lined up on her arm, while another sat in a booth, on break, looking out the window. Her legs were crossed, and her arms were wrapped tightly around herself. She had a plateful of food before her, but she stared out at the rain.

Dennis photographed waitresses with hair fashioned into falling-down ponytails or sprayed-up beehives or neat little short dos,

some of which were festooned with bows or barrettes; it's astonishing
to me how clearly I recall those images, now. You could see such weariness in the set of shoulders. You could see blatant invitation in the
thrusting forward of breasts. You could see a handkerchief pinned
above a pocket, an emphatic smear of eye shadow, a run in a nylon, a
thin arm that reached for a pile of coins left beneath a tabletop juke-
box.

I write:

*I have books of photography by Dorothea Lange and Walker
Evans, because their work reminds me of you. One of Evans's
images I've been looking at lately is of a grave situated at the
edge of a field that stretches far out, row after row of tilled earth,
five telephone poles running alongside. And it was the telephone
wires that got me. Life going on above, chatter along the lines;
below . . . who knew?*

*I had an abstract fear of death when I was young. These days,
it is not so abstract, but then it is not so much a fear anymore,
either. You used to say, "When it's time to come in, it's time to
come in, that's all." And I remember you quite naturally
subscribed to the idea of communication after death, something I
have never believed in more than now.*

*You ask how I am. Well enough, is the short answer. The
world is more complex than I once believed; people are, too. I
write books that I hope will help people with various problems in
their lives, and I give a lot of talks all over the country, and
occasionally abroad. Hearing from you has made me realize
something: oftentimes, when I give talks, I'm sharing knowledge I
gained from being with you. And I'm trying to motivate people in
the same way that you tried to motivate me: to be awake, to stay*

true, to evolve. The friend I just lost was like you in that way, too:
you would have liked each other, I think.

Are you married? I'm not. Whether you are or not, I am
excited at the prospect of having you, however tangentially, in my
life again.

Why are you in Cleveland? Now that you are closer, I'd like to
come and visit you there. Or perhaps you would like to come
here?

Dennis Halsinger. I think it is not much of an exaggeration to
say that I remember everything.

> Yours,
> Cece

I add a P.S. with my cellphone number, then put the pen down and
stare at the letter. What can this mean, this great excitement, this
overwhelming desire to see him? I suppose that for one thing, it
means I need someone I can talk to, talk to *really*. This is the first
time since Penny died that I've wanted to. "Okay, Penny," I say.
"When is now. I'm going to make a move."

It's about time.

"I wish you'd known him," I tell her.

Oh I know him, now.

LAST SEPTEMBER, BEFORE PENNY WAS DIAGNOSED, THERE WAS an unseasonably cold Sunday near the end of the month. Snow was predicted, though it never came. Penny and I were sitting out on her front porch under electric blankets, leafing through our respective backlogs of magazines. "You know what you are?" she said.

"What?" I asked, barely looking up from my magazine.

"A flaming hypocrite."

Now I did look up. "*Flaming*, huh?"

"Yes." She flipped a couple pages of her magazine. Angrily, I thought.

"What's your problem?" I asked.

She looked over at me. "My problem is that you tell other people how to do things you yourself need to do, and don't. You write books for other people full of advice that you never follow."

"Now, now. You know what they say in couples therapy about the use of *always* and *never*."

"Yeah, well, we're not a couple. We're best friends. Supposedly."

I sighed. "Okay. You want to talk again about how we need to travel somewhere together?"

"No. I want to talk about how you say you want to simplify your life, how you want to downsize, and clarify what's important, and do what you really need to do, and then you . . . don't."

I sat there for a moment, then said, "Is this about the bamboo sheets I just ordered?" There'd been an 800 number in one of the magazines.

Nothing.

"I wanted those sheets. They're really beautiful and they feel—"

"You have bamboo sheets."

"Not in light green. I have them in white and light blue."

"How many do you need?"

"Listen, Penny, I work hard. As you know. I like nice things. I can afford nice things. And so I buy them. Okay? I like to own nice things."

"They own you. You don't stop working so much because you have to keep making money to pay for things you buy that you do *not* need."

I looked at her. Licked my lips and pushed my hair back off my shoulders. "Let me ask you something."

"Ask."

"Do you need everything you've got?"

"No. No! And that's why I'm getting rid of it! You just helped me fill up all those bags of clothes to give away. And I've brought nearly all the stuff I had in the attic to Goodwill."

"Where, next time we go, you'll buy it all back," I said.

"No, I won't. In case you haven't noticed, Miss Perceptive, I have not been buying much of anything but groceries."

"Well, good for you. Why don't you get rid of *everything* you don't need?"

"I *will*. That's my *goal*. I don't want these . . . *things* anymore. They're an unnecessary complication. A hindrance."

"You know what? You're the hypocrite, Penny. You will never give away all the stuff you don't need! Look at all the kitchen toys you have. I never saw anyone with more kitchen toys than you, and you hardly ever even cook! Why don't you give away one of your precious Microplanes? You have three different sizes!"

"I gave them all away."

"What? To whom?"

"To Kate Webster, who loves them and who cooks a lot and will use them."

I sniffed. "You might have asked me. I would have wanted them."

"Why? You cook less often than I!"

"I just like them. I would have wanted them."

Penny shook her head. "For a smart woman, you are really dense. You just keep on. . . . And here's another thing. What about how you say you want a meaningful and lasting relationship? What do you do about that?"

"Hasn't worked out."

"You don't let it work out!"

Silence.

Then, more gently, she said, "What about that hippy-dippy love affair you had, that guy you never got over?"

"Who, Dennis Halsinger?"

"Yeah."

"He's not here."

"Well, he's not dead!"

"Well, he's not here."

"Well . . . *Google* him!"

"I've tried! He's not . . . Googleable! And anyway, what good would it do? He's in Tahiti!"

"You are so stubborn. When are you going to see that you keep moving in the wrong direction to get the things you say you really want?"

"I suppose when Miss *Guru* finally gets through to me."

"I'm saying this for your benefit, you asshole!"

I threw down my magazine. "You know, Penny, you are not your-self lately. I don't know if you need more sleep or what, but you are not yourself. You're always so pissed off!"

She looked down. "I know. I don't feel good. I'm going to the doc-tor tomorrow to get some tests done. I'm probably anemic or some-thing. I'm tired all the time."

Three days later, she walked in my door and said, "Come and sit down with me. I've got something to tell you."

We cried, of course, both of us. We talked statistics, prognoses. I saw that my hands were shaking and I made them stop. I asked her, "What should I do for you?"

She shrugged. "I don't know, be with me, I guess, as much as you can."

"Do you want to go somewhere? Do you want to take a road trip?"

Her answer was in her smile: *too late.* But then she said, "You know what you can do for me? Use your skills in some meaningful way right here instead of running all over the country. Slow down, step back, be inside your own skin, *live.* Open yourself to love. And give back in some meaningful way!"

I sat still, listening.

Then she said, "I think you should volunteer at the Arms."

"What's that?"

"It's a hospice in Saint Paul. They do really good work. I thought about going there when I . . . I thought about going there but Brice and I decided I'd stay home."

"A *hospice*?" I said.

"Will you do it?"

"Oh God, that would be so—" I stopped myself, but she knew what I'd been going to say.

"It's not depressing," she said. "It's a very life-affirming place. I promise you."

"Yes," I told her. "Yes, I will volunteer at the Arms. And I'll . . . I'll work on doing all those other things, too."

"Promise?"

"Promise."

She smiled and leaned back in the chair.

I did stay with her as much as I could. I went with her to medical appointments and we always did something fun afterward—once it was trying on ridiculous evening wear. We did the things we used to do, too—we went to movies and browsed in stores, we had lunch out in pretty restaurants, we got pedicures, and we sat on a bench by the lake and fed the ducks. Finally, it got too hard for her to go out: she'd be worn out by the time she buttoned her coat. So we stayed in. We watched movies on television, we played cards. And we talked. Mostly it was about things we'd always talked about: what was in the paper, books, dreams, Brice, her nutty brother. But once she said, "Remember when we were packing up my clothes to give away, how I'd said that moving forward, I just wanted to travel lighter? Well. Be careful what you wish for, right?"

Then we talked about what it might be like, dying. Being dead. Whether either of us truly believed in a kind of awareness after death. I said I did, but I wouldn't look at her, saying it. But then when she said she did, too, I did look at her, and it felt to me like we made some sort of promise to each other. It was on that day, too, that she said, "Remember when we went to that Weight Watchers meeting and they told us that the time to stop eating was when you still wanted a little more? Maybe it's good for me to go now. I won't get old and start losing everything. You know, my sight. My hearing. My marbles. I won't be wishing I'd die, already."

"True," I said, and I tried to latch on to that fragile optimism. But I couldn't. I didn't want her to go. I wanted us to get old together and complain to each other about our aching joints and failing memories, the many pills that we had to take every day. I wanted her and Brice and me to continue to be next-door neighbors in some old-age community, where we'd sit out by the garden with blankets on our laps until they called us in for dinner.

On the last day, I came over in the morning and she'd gotten quite bad; her breathing was rough. I knelt by the bed and took her hands in mine, and she said, "Oh, my wonderful . . ." Her face changed then, I saw a soft regret, and she said, "Just Brice, now. Okay?"

"Okay," I said, and I kissed her forehead and said, "See you."

I went downstairs and waited out the final hours there. It was right for her to be with just Brice, I honored that request in my head and in my heart. I have also never in my life felt so bitterly isolated. I was sleeping on the sofa with a magazine in my hand when Brice came down and tapped me on the shoulder. My eyes flew open. He nodded. He was in his stocking feet, his shirt twisted off to one side. His face looked like it had been delicately, gingerly put into place, as though it were ready to fall off, or break apart into a million pieces.

"What time is it?" I asked, absurdly.

He looked at his watch. "Four-seventeen?"

We stared at each other and then we both burst into tears.

I went home and sat at my kitchen table and resolved to do every single thing she'd asked me to do. And then I am sorry to say that I did not.

Now, finally, I will. Now I can. I haven't yet committed to the last speaking engagement I was offered. I just turned in my latest book. I can take a break. I can, in fact, stop altogether, if I want to.

I go to my computer and get the number for the Arms. I'll make an appointment for an interview, just to get a sense of the place, just to see what I might be able to offer—and, to be honest, to see if I *can* offer anything. Then I'll call a realtor to come and see my house, and I'll start looking for another place to live.

Perhaps most important, I'll find a way to see Dennis. It comes to me that hearing from him is what has loosened the lynchpin, and that even if nothing else happens with him, I owe him a debt of gratitude for that.

I breathe out, and feel a kind of lightness move into me. It appears that what I wrote in my last book is true: *Once you start making decisions in which your heart, mind, and soul are congruent, you'll feel it as a kind of lift, if not liftoff.*

SATURDAY MORNING, I FIND A PLACE TO PARK DIRECTLY IN front of HavenCrest, where my mother lives. I go into the lobby and greet the few people I see there. Then I head up to my mother's apartment, the last one at the end of a long hall, so she has a great view of the woods that surround this place, and the little creek that runs behind it. Walking down the hall, I feel a kind of envy. She did it. She moved into a much smaller place; it's all done, and she's thriving.

"It's open!" she calls when I knock on the door.

She comes out of the bathroom with one eyebrow drawn in, one to go. She must have just had her hair done; it curls nicely along the sides of her face, bringing out her still-lovely cheekbones. She's wearing a blue dress that matches her eyes, and a gold bracelet and earrings. She has on her fancy orthopedic shoes that hardly look like orthopedic shoes at all: they're a kind of Mary Jane. The place must be having one of its events, an ice cream social, perhaps. I hug her and her head barely comes up to the middle of my chest; I think she must have shrunk again.

"I'm just putting my face on," she tells me. "Wait for me in the kitchen. There's coffee cake. Say hello to your father."

I go into the kitchen and sit down at the little table, which is set for two. My father died three years ago, but my mother still sets a place for him, still talks to him, still feels his presence. I sit at the table opposite his place, see how she's put the sports page next to his plate as usual, folded the way he liked to do it.

"Hi, Dad," I say to the empty chair.

My mother comes into the kitchen. "Cup of coffee?"

"No thanks."

"What are you doing here?"

"Nice to see *you,* too."

"Well, it's always nice to see you, you know that. But you never come in the morning. And why aren't you in Cincinnati? Is something wrong?"

"It was Atlanta, and I got home yesterday."

"Oh, for heaven's sake, I know you went to Atlanta. I have a date; I'm a little nervous. When I get nervous, I forget everything."

"You have a date?"

"Does that happen to you? When you get nervous, does everything just fly out of your brain?"

"Yes, Mom. But . . . did you say you have a date?"

"I'm just going out to lunch with Spencer Thompson. You know Spencer, the big ears. We're just going over to the Olive Garden. We've got coupons ready to expire."

"The Olive Garden where you and Dad used to go all the time?"

"Yes. And never mind, your father thinks it's just fine. It was his idea! But how was your talk?"

"It was great. The women were really nice. So, Mom, are you—"

"Did you bring me the amenities?"

I pull out a plastic bag from my purse, and show her the lotion and shampoo, the shower cap and cream rinse and mouthwash.

"Good girl. You know, I use those shower caps to cover leftovers. They work just great!"

She's told me this at least two hundred times.

Now she'll tell me how the products in the little containers are superior to those in the big containers. She'll tell me that that's how they get you to buy the big size, which is then watered down.

But that's not what happens. What happens is, she sits opposite me and says, "Are you still thinking of selling your house?"

"Who said that?"

"You did, last time you were here."

"Oh." I'd forgotten all about it.

"Well," I say, "it seems as though it's time. I'm reminded of Penny too much, living there. And I really want to downsize. I'm going to look for a smaller place."

"Oh, honey, I'm glad. You'll be surprised at how freeing it is. And here's the thing. Bess Templeton told me that her granddaughter is looking for a roommate. She has a lovely house over by Como Park. One of the women who lived there just moved out."

"Yeah, I don't think I can live with roommates again, though. I don't think I'd want to do that. But thanks for—"

"I'm just saying you might consider it. Why go somewhere and live all by yourself again? I worry about you getting lonely, with Penny gone."

"I'll be fine," I tell her, but the truth is, she's right. I already am lonely.

"Let me go over to Bess's and get the address. *If* the place is still available. Apparently, it's real cute. 'Just darling!' Bess said. And one of the women who lives there is a chef!"

Well, my mother knows how to play her cards. I love to eat and I don't really like cooking that much, especially when it's just for me.

"I'll be right back. Talk to your father."

After my mother leaves, I look around her kitchen, thinking of how difficult it was for her when she moved out of her beloved house and into this place a few years ago, though she never complained. It must have been a hard adjustment, complicated by the fact that my father had just died. But now she really likes it here.

In a couple of minutes she's back, handing me a piece of paper with an address in Saint Paul. "The room is still available, but Bess said they're meeting with someone who might rent it this morning. She called and made an appointment for you this afternoon. She told them not to make a decision until they'd met you."

"Mom. I—"

"Oh, just go over and meet the people. What have you got to lose? It might just be an option to consider until you decide what you *really* want to do."

This is codespeak for settle down and get married, which my mother has been waiting for me to do for . . . well, I would say since I was born.

My mother looks at her watch. "You'd better go, you don't want to be late."

"Where's the phone number? I should call and cancel; I'm really not comfortable with this idea."

"I don't think she gave me the phone number," my mother says, a tad vaguely, and before I can accuse her of purposefully not taking it, she says, "Is my lipstick in the lines?"

I lean forward to look and tell her that it is. This makes for a little prick of tenderness in my heart and now I can't yell at her for trying to help me.

"Let me know how it goes," she says, as I pick up my purse to head out.

"Yeah you too," I say. "Have a nice time on your date."

My mother puts her finger to her lips and points to my dad's chair. I smile. "You said it was his idea!"

I ARRIVE HALF AN HOUR EARLY TO THE NEIGHBORHOOD IN SAINT Paul where the house is. I spot a coffee shop and am about to go in when my cellphone rings. It's Brice.

"Hey!" I say. "How are you?"

"Good, good; how about you, sweetheart?"

"I'm okay. Considering."

He sighs. "Yeah. I know."

"Are you doing okay?"

"Well, actually, I'm calling to tell you that I . . . met someone."

I stop breathing.

"She's not Penny. But she's really great. And we just decided to get married."

"Oh, wow."

"And I wanted to tell you because . . ."

I manage to say, "I'm glad for you, Brice."

"Really?"

"Yes. Really."

"Good. I guess that's why I was calling. I guess I wanted your permission or your blessing or something. I thought about waiting longer, but . . ."

"You know what Penny used to tell me all the time, Brice?"

"What?"

"*People with people, good. People alone, bad.* Over and over. She told me that all the time."

"She did tell me she wanted me to get married again."

"And I'll bet she didn't say a thing about waiting."

"No, she didn't. She told me to do it right away, in fact. Anyway. Thanks, Cece. I wanted to tell you first because you and Penny were . . ."

My eyes fill. "Yes. We were."

"So."

"So! When's the wedding?"

"Two weeks. Would you . . . ? You don't want to come, do you?"

"Oh! Thanks. But . . . no."

"How's everything else? How are things with you and the dentist?"

"The dentist?"

"Yeah, isn't your boyfriend a dentist?"

"Seamus? No, he's a carpenter."

"A carpenter! Right! I wonder why I said 'dentist.'"

"I don't know. They both have drills?"

He laughs. "Probably. So are things good with you and him?"

"Well, we, you know . . . we kind of broke up."

"I'm sorry. Penny thought maybe he was the one for you."

"Yeah. Almost!"

I look out the side window, where two women are getting out of their car and going into the coffee shop. They're laughing so hard one of them has to stop walking.

"Listen, I'm just on my way to an appointment," I say. "But I'm really glad for you. Be happy, okay?"

"Thank you. And, Cece?"

"Yes?"

"I just want to . . . You know, I'm sure, that she wanted so much for you to be with someone."

"I know."

"I do, too, sweetheart. I've learned it's not so good to be alone. I don't know how you've done it all these years."

I did it day by day, I want to tell him. Month by month. And then year by year. I decided in high school that I wasn't going to get married too soon. I'd forgotten that you can also wait too long, and then the only candies left in the box are the squished ones, rejected for their questionable insides. And if I am honest, I'd have to count myself among those with questionable insides. As Penny was fond of reminding me, I've never been able to make that particular leap of faith, to find within myself the kind of trust that exchanging vows requires. Though I did have a friend whose fiancé insisted that the old vows be used, and when the minister asked if she promised to "honor and obey," she burst out laughing.

It's a cliché based on enough truth to have made it a cliché: the wistful bridesmaids, straining to catch the flung bouquet. But I was always the bridesmaid who stood at the back with my arms crossed, a little insulted that I had to even pretend I wanted it. I watched many happy couples drive away, vastly relieved that I was free and not the one stepping into that decorated vehicle.

"You know, marriage is what you and your husband make of it," Penny once told me. "You don't have to cleave to anyone else's paradigm."

"I know that," I said.

And she said, "I'm not sure you do."

Now I tell Brice, "I'm thinking about moving somewhere else, maybe in with other people."

"Really?"

"Yeah, maybe. I'm trying to stay open to a lot of possibilities, including not knowing yet what all those possibilities might be."

"You're not going to give me one of your lectures now, are you? You're not going to ask me to take out a piece of paper and write down the first word that occurs to me and drop it in the basket, are you?" This was a technique I used sometimes in workshops.

"Not unless you pay me."

He laughs. "I miss you, Cece."

"You, too."

"Keep in touch. Drop me an email now and then."

"I will."

But I don't think we'll email anymore. He's moved on in a way I can't, yet. It occurs to me that I should have asked about his new wife. I wish she could know one thing about Penny. When it became absolutely clear that she was not going to experience the miracle cure we all prayed for, Penny embarked on a daunting task: she wiped out and lined every drawer and cupboard in her house with beautiful paper. When I asked why she was using up so much of the limited energy she had on this, she said, "I want it to be nice for Brice's next wife."

I go into the coffee shop and order a coffee and a mini-cupcake. I find a table and drink my coffee and watch the people in the shop. I smell the beans being ground, listen to snippets of conversation and bursts of laughter. But on the inside, I tell Penny that Brice is getting married.

I know.

I bite into my cupcake and tell Penny that I know she wanted Brice to remarry, but now that he's really doing it, doesn't it hurt her feelings?

No. It's bigger, here.

I check my watch, refill my coffee cup, sit back down at the table, and while I pretend to read a newspaper someone has left behind, I tell Penny about the letters Dennis Halsinger used to send me. At first they were written on napkins, the envelopes made out of magazine pages and sealed with masking tape, and I relished the quirky artistry of that, even copied it for a while. Then, as he began to make some money, the letters came on tissue-thin pages with rambling, poetic passages about what he was seeing and feeling: the incredible natural beauty of Tahiti, the politics of the place; the way he evolved in his views of what love and life were meant to be. I remember lying on my bed and reading his response to one of my letters where I despaired of ever finding true and lasting love. He said love only made sense in the context of it being in your own mind first, then given to others; that trying to force it never worked.

Go and see him. Just get in the car and do it.

I hear it as clearly as if she has spoken it right into my ear.

Do it!

"I will!" I say. The people sitting at the table next to me look over at me, then away.

FIND THE HOUSE WITH THE ROOM FOR RENT EASILY, WHITE stucco with a red lacquered door. It's pretty, but the yard needs tending, and the house could use a coat of paint. There's a big front porch with both a hammock and a swing, wicker chairs with faded floral-print pillows, the chairs angled toward each other as though they are having a conversation. Between them is a wicker table with a lamp, and anchored to the wall behind it is a long white shelf holding an assemblage of paperbacks. In a corner of the porch is an antique wrought-iron tea cart, seriously off-balance, but with coffee mugs and a few wineglasses turned upside down on a dishcloth anyway. Even with its imperfections—or maybe because of them—it's a charming exterior, welcoming.

I take a quick walk along the side of the house to look at the backyard. It's huge, much bigger than you'd think from the street. There's a small garden there, but it's ill tended. I think, *If I live here and if they want me to, I'll fix it up.* I'll plant cosmos and bearded iris, hot pink roses, Stargazer lilies and tree peonies. Maybe a bank of Miss Kim lilacs along the back fence, and some climbing hydrangea to grow up the side of the house. I'd love to have forget-me-nots, too, and daisies, and the exotic purple globes of allium. There's room for a big vegetable garden. There could even be a space for meditation, off in one corner.

More than the glorious bounty, I realize I'd like the gratification of doing the labor that a garden requires. I like nestling young plants into warm earth. I even like the sight of fat earthworms turning the soil inches from my hand. I like getting tired and dirty for such a good reason.

Well. I'm getting a little ahead of myself.

I go back around to the front and knock on the door. I hear a dog barking and a voice telling him to hush. Then the door is opened by a woman in her late forties, early fifties, with wild blond curls and bright blue eyes. She's wearing a long skirt, a lacy top, and hoop earrings. "Oh, hi, I'm Joni," she says. "Are you Cecilia?" She's out of breath and a little excited.

"I am!" I like friendly people like this who immediately make you feel welcome, and quite pleased to be yourself.

An ancient yellow Lab with a solid white muzzle races over to sniff at my pants leg. "No, no, Riley, don't!" Joni says, grabbing his collar. Then, to me, "He'll calm right down. He's such a busybody, master of the house, you know." She stands aside. "Anyway. Come in! We were just about to have lunch, will you join us? I made a cheese soufflé and a spinach salad with strawberries and candied walnuts."

An interview with benefits, it seems. Why not. "Sounds great," I say.

As we pass the living room, I see comfortable-looking furniture, a kind of shabby-chic look with an off-white sofa you just want to fall into. There's a flat-screen TV, a fireplace with a blue stone surround that looks like lapis lazuli, and an overcrowded bookcase, my favorite kind. Nice artwork, which looks to be original, and a large, glass-topped oval coffee table holding oversize books and a tray with a vintage martini pitcher and glass. The pitcher has a bouquet of yellow tulips in it, and the martini glass holds jacks and a red rubber ball. I see jewel-tone pillows stacked in the corner, and assume they are used if people want to eat around that table. There's a chaise lounge by the window, a reading lamp beside it. Two off-white overstuffed armchairs with hassocks.

"Come and meet the others," Joni says. "They're at the table. In the dining room. Right in here. Follow me!"

We go into the dining room, where the wooden floor is covered by a faded Oriental rug in tones of pink, blue, and cream. There is a beamed ceiling, those beams painted a soft white, and the room is well lit by a bank of high art-glass windows. The large round antique oak table has been nicely restored, and above it hangs a chandelier featuring glass birds that I think I once saw in an Anthropologie store. I had looked at it for a long time; I'd almost bought it, but I had nowhere to put it. It looks perfect here. A sign, I think, that chandelier being here.

"So, this is Cecilia," Joni tells the two women sitting at the table. Then, pointing to the younger, dark-haired woman, "That's Renie. Well, Irene, but Renie."

"Hi," I say, and Renie raises a hand, stays silent. She reminds me of a bird: close-cropped hair like a chickadee's cap, a delicate frame, a sharp nose, large round eyes. She's wearing an open, blue-checked flannel shirt over a gray T-shirt, blue jeans. She has a diamond nose stud.

"And this is Lise," Joni says, pointing to the other woman at the table, fortyish with dark brown eyes behind wire-rimmed glasses. Her light brown hair is pulled into a ponytail and she's wearing a crisp white blouse and gray linen slacks. She exudes a kind of grace and calm, but it's mixed with a watchfulness that makes her a cat to Renie's bird.

"Hi, Cecilia," Lise says, and her voice is warm.

"It's Lise's house," Joni says. "Maybe you knew that already, did you know that already?"

"My house, but unequivocally Joni's kitchen," Lise says. "Welcome!" She holds her hand out to shake mine and I am struck by the length of her fingers. "Pianist?" I ask, and she smiles. "Physician. I'm in family practice at HealthPartners. I'm afraid the only instrument I play is a rubber band."

"Let me show you the room real quick," Joni says, "and then we'll have lunch."

We climb the stairs and go past a large bathroom with a claw-foot tub, vintage black and white tiles. There's a white bureau against the wall, bath products arranged on the top like a glass bouquet, and I imagine there are towels in the drawers. In the corner is a birdcage on a stand, a pink flowering plant inside.

The room for rent is the last room on the right. It's very large, painted a cream color with white trim, egg-and-dart molding. The sun shines in brightly; the floor is polished to a high sheen. There's a window seat that overlooks the backyard. And just like that: I know. I want to live here. Attached as I am to my house, I don't want to be there anymore. I want to move on. I want to be here, in a new place, with new people, with a new garden to put in. And with nothing to do but fix up my own bedroom.

I turn to Joni. "I love it."

She beams. "Right? It's the nicest bedroom, really," she says. "It was Sandy's, Lise's daughter." She lowers her voice to say, "I wouldn't mention her. They don't get along."

Joni stands with her arms crossed, looking around. "There really is a nice feeling to this room, it's such a nice feeling. We're all too lazy to move, or we'd be fighting over it. Okay, let's eat." Over her shoulder she adds, "Those are my three favorite words."

On the way to the dining room, she takes me past a powder room with black and white polka-dotted wallpaper and a cherry-red toilet seat, then into the large kitchen, which is magnificent: a true chef's kitchen complete with a six-burner stove and a butcher block island, above which are hanging many pots and pans. Next to the window, there's a vinyl booth with a semicircular, tuck-and-roll bench, the kind you might find in a diner, and it is full of pillows, which appear to have been made from vintage embroidered dishtowels, the kind that designate a job for each day of the week: Monday, washing; Tuesday, ironing; and so forth.

During lunch, I learn that Joni is a widow, and a lunchtime sous-chef at Ultramarine, which is one of the fanciest restaurants—if not *the* fanciest restaurant—in the Twin Cities.

"Ultramarine!" I say.

"Ultramarine," she says back, sighing.

"Just when I was starting to like you," I say. "Now I'm going to have to be afraid of you."

"Oh, you don't have to be afraid of me. I'm Jekyll here, Hyde there. That's the problem with pressure cooker restaurants like that. The only civilized part is the staff meal before we start work. Have you eaten there?"

I shake my head. "Not yet." I don't like restaurants where you have to take out a second mortgage to pay the check.

"Come in someday and I'll treat you," Joni says. "I'll have to seat you by the kitchen. And then you'll hear the sound of hair being ripped out of heads, but the meal will be fantastic!"

"What compels you to work in a place like that?" I ask.

She looks at me. "It's *Ultramarine*." She shrugs. "Plus I lose weight, working there. I must sweat off a pound an hour. But it's getting to me. I'm not as young as I used to be, as they say. When you do what I do, fifty-two feels like ninety-two."

"I keep telling you you should do yoga," Lise tells her. "It would help you. It really helps me. And it's good exercise."

"You're ten years younger than I am," Joni says. "That's what helps you."

"Yoga is not exercise," Renie says. "It is a thinly disguised competition where people are judged on their personalized mats and cute little yoga outfits and ability to act like a heron or the letter *Q*."

"That is not true," Lise says. "Why don't you try it sometime? You can come with me any Friday for a free session."

"Yeah, I'd love to, but I have an appointment every Friday."

"When?"

"All day and all night. It's a very unusual appointment." Renie turns to me. "What do you think, is yoga exercise?"

My mouth is full of salad. I hold up my palms: *Beats me*.

"A diplomat," Renie says. "How boring."

I've learned that Renie works for an alternative newspaper. She was a reporter at the *Star Tribune*, but after she did a satirical piece on advice columns, she was hired by *In a Different Voice* to do a regular column that she calls "Get Over Yourself." She reminds me of a Tarot card called the King of Wands, which signifies someone tough on the outside, tender on the inside. Well, I like a challenge. If I live here, I'll figure out a way into her. And if not, I think the other two will make up for her.

Lise, who is divorced, owns not only the house but the dog. She told me she decided to rent out rooms after her only child moved out. "Her name is Sandy," Lise said. "She's twenty. She lives in Dinkytown and goes to the University of Minnesota. She's pretty busy over there; I don't really see her that much."

I nod, like it's all new to me. Joni stares at her plate.

"I really like the people who have lived here," Lise says. "And I get free dog- and house-sitting when I travel. You do like dogs, don't you?"

"Love them!" I say.

Lise pushes her chair back from the table. "Well, I don't know about the rest of you, but I'm ready to cast my vote right now, for yes." She looks at me. "That is, if you are agreeable to moving in."

I'm a little surprised that she's asked me this so suddenly, but maybe she's like me: when she knows, she knows. I really like the bedroom, I like the whole house, I love the neighborhood, and I'm intrigued by the mix of ages and occupations of the women who live here.

"I do have to ask one thing," I say. "Would it be all right if I put in a garden? Flowers, vegetables, maybe a space for meditation?"

"I'd be grateful," Lise says. "It's a mess out there. Do whatever you like!"

"A space for *meditation*?" Renie says.

I ignore her. "I could do some pots for your front porch, too. I was thinking dahlia and blue ageratum, maybe some verbena and lemon licorice?"

"Oh wow, what a great idea," Joni says. "That would be so pretty!"

"And I can move in right away, if that makes any difference." I sit still, waiting for the others to speak.

No problem as far as Joni is concerned: she claps her hands and says, "Fine with me. I can't wait for the vegetable garden. We should put in herbs, too."

Renie looks down at her lap. "Why don't we talk about it later?"

"Come on," Lise says. "Let's just vote her in. I'm tired of doing interviews."

Renie looks at me. "All right. No offense, but I don't think you're a good fit. A motivational speaker who writes self-help books?"

"*Renie,*" Joni says.

Lise says, "I've read one of her books, and it was really good."

"Really?" I say, and so does Renie, though with an entirely different tone.

"You read a *self-help* book?" Renie asks Lise.

"Yes, Renie, I read a *self-help* book, and guess what? It helped!" She turns to me. "It was quite useful to me after my divorce."

"Thank you. I'm glad."

Renie readjusts herself in her chair. "We agreed that we all have to agree, right?"

No one says anything.

I reach for my purse. "Well, thanks for considering me. I enjoyed the lunch."

"Tell you what," Renie says. "Why don't you see if you can *motivate* me to get up out of my chair? If you can, it's fine with me if you move in."

"Stop it, Renie," Lise says.

"Oh, come on, it'll be fun. It'll be like *The Sword in the Stone* or something."

"What is *wrong* with you?" Joni asks. "You know, you're the real reason Vicky moved out. She would have stayed if it weren't for you. You're why she moved out. So."

"Thanks again," I say, starting to get up. And then I fall to the floor. Everyone leaps up.

"Oh my God, are you all right?" Joni asks.

I get on my feet and look at Renie, who is standing opposite me. "Well. Looks like you're out of your chair."

The other women laugh, and Renie sits back down, her arms crossed tightly over her chest. "How old are you, anyway?"

Well, now she's gotten me mad. I have a problem with ageism, overt and especially covert. My feeling about a person's age is that it's a serving suggestion. It's up to you what you do with it: take it as offered, modify it, or ignore it altogether.

"How old are *you*?" I ask.

"I'm thirty-nine. And I'm gay."

"So fucking what?"

"Oh, she's in," Joni says. "Don't you think so? Isn't she in, Renie?"

I take a step closer. "I'm a good person. I'm fair, I'm honest, I'm responsible, I'm not moody. I take short showers and I'm terrific at organizing. I don't mind cleaning; in fact, I like cleaning. I even like cleaning out the refrigerator. *And* I can fix a running toilet."

Renie smiles. "You want me to help you get your bed over here? I have a truck. Then, later tonight, we can all lie out under the stars holding hands and sharing our innermost *thoughts and feelings.*"

"Sounds great," I say. "And look how far ahead of the game *you* are al*ready*!"

WHEN I GET HOME, I CALL THE REAL ESTATE AGENCY NEAR-
est me and make an appointment to have my house listed. And then
I feel a sudden pang of sadness: I'd been wondering when it would
hit. Sure as I am that I want to leave, it will be hard to sell this house.

I go upstairs and into my bedroom closet to take out my box of
fortunes, as I call it. I open it and see the worn deck of Tarot cards
that Cosmina gave me, and the burgundy velvet bag holding glass
stones, Runes, upon which are etched letters from an ancient alpha-
betic script. There's the venerable *I Ching,* which Dennis taught me
to use so many years ago, and a collection of cards a woman who came
to a talk once gave me. They feature images of flowers, and have
evocative words and definitions torn from the dictionary on the bot-
toms. She also gave me cards with images of women, and on the bot-
toms of those are various fragments or statements, things like: *It was
the one, true thing to do.*

There's one deck of divinatory cards that are my favorites, in part
because they're so fast: I form a question and spread the cards out in
my hand with the images facing away from me. I close my eyes and
wait to feel as though a card is asking me to pick it. Sometimes it's
immediate; sometimes it takes longer, but always, always, the feeling
comes to draw a particular one. And then I use the book to interpret
the meaning of the card I've drawn. There's a brief summary of what

the image represents, a story that is "the teaching," and finally "the application," so that you can incorporate that teaching into your life.

Cosmina was right when she suggested I had no psychic ability. But I believe these cards and other tools help me to understand myself in some deeper way. I have used them for guidance on important matters far more often than I would admit to just anyone. Penny knew, of course; she was my partner in mystical inquiry and in interpretation. We always went out on my porch for our readings, regardless of the season. Porch Tellers, I called us.

Now I take my box to the front porch and pull out my favorite deck of cards. They still carry the scent of the incense sold in the store where I bought them, a little place in New Orleans that I found when I gave a talk there. It was a dark and narrow place, both peaceful and charged. Just walking in there made you feel enlivened in a particular way, as though you were outlined by something that glowed.

I sit down in one of the chairs, try to ignore the other one, which Penny always sat in. I spread the cards out in my hand, close my eyes, and pose this question: *Should I really sell my house and move in with those other women?*

I sit still and wait for the pull. There. I feel it. I reach to the right, put my hand on a card, hesitate, and then pull the one beneath it. I open my eyes and see that I've gotten the fertility card. I don't ever recall having pulled it before. The application says, *You are being asked to rebirth yourself, to bring new life to an old and stagnant place.* Then, toward the end, *If you are considering beginning something new, the time is right. It is in you to succeed, if you choose to. Leave behind what has held you back, and move forward with confidence and joy.*

I sit thinking for a moment. Then I consult the Book of Runes to see if I get the same kind of answer. This method uses three Runes that you pull from the velvet pouch with your eyes closed and lay in a row before you. For most Runes, the meaning changes depending on whether you lay the stone right side up or upside down; very few read the same both ways. The stones address three things: the situation as it is, the challenge, and the outcome.

The first Rune I draw is Gebo, which signifies two things: *partnership* and *a gift*. The text says, *Drawing this Rune is an indication that union, uniting, and partnership in some form is at hand.* Further on, it says, *This counsel applies at all levels: in love relationships, in business affairs, in partnering of every kind. It is particularly appropriate when entering into partnership with what some call your Higher Self.*

Finally, I pull one of my "women" cards, which shows someone looking upward, as if in entreaty, with roses cascading from her hair. There is a clock below her, and the statement is *Time is making her decision for her.*

Well, that's enough for me. I return my things to the box, carry it upstairs, and put it on the floor beside my bed. I don't want to forget it when I move.

I put on jeans and a sweatshirt, and I give the house a good cleaning. Scrubbing behind the toilet, I think of my co-worker, Mike Adams. When he and his wife put their house on the market, they cleaned in a way they never had before. And he said, "Man, if I'd known it could look this good, I'd have kept it like this all the time. Betsy even put fresh flowers in the bathrooms!"

At precisely four o'clock, just after I've changed into decent clothes, the doorbell rings. The realtor's name is Marilyn Watson, and she has a great reputation for selling houses quickly. Her face is on bus stop benches, which I've always thought of as superstardom for real estate agents. She's wearing a bright red power suit with big gold buttons, and her blond hair is sprayed into a formidable updo.

"I just love this block," she says. "And what a garden you have out front!"

"Wait till you see the back."

I take Marilyn for a tour of the house, and in doing so I fully realize that what is here is not just things: good-size rooms, furniture, draperies, rugs, books, dishes. What's here are the selves I've been since I moved here when I was thirty years old. So many intentions and aspirations I had, moving in. Many were realized, some were not.

As Marilyn inspects the bedroom, I lean against the wall, my hands flat on the surface. There is something that many carpenters do when they put up new walls: they nestle things into the insulation. It could be a page from a newspaper, a beer bottle, a new penny. Seamus, my carpenter, used to put poems there. He had an Irishman's love for the form, and he used to read poems to me in bed. Sometimes I would fall asleep to them, and I still recommend it as the best way to enter into your dreams, *to mount the black horse for the deep ride,* Seamus used to call going to sleep. It was typical of him to say something like that, something half sarcastic and half sincere. In the end, when our times together became less about poetry and more about argument, I accused him of being someone who was afraid to stand behind his own convictions. He accused me of the same thing.

I slept with him many times in this room. The last time he stayed with me, I held him in my arms and looked up at the ceiling, wondering who would be the first to say it was over. It was a rainy night and we'd made meatballs and spaghetti for dinner in our pajamas and there'd hung over our gay preparation a knowing pall.

That night he'd read me a poem that he was going to put behind the wall of a remodeled bedroom of a couple who'd been married for sixty-seven years. They needed their doorway widened to accommodate the wheelchair the man was now in. They hired an architect of great renown and redid the whole bedroom beautifully. I loved the poem Seamus used for them so much that I made a copy of it, and I've practically memorized it. It's by Ellen Bass, and it's called "Gate C22." It's about an older man kissing an older woman who is just off a plane. The ending goes:

> *you once lay there, the vernix*
> *not yet wiped off, and someone gazed at you*
> *as if you were the first sunrise seen from the Earth.*

But that night when Seamus read it to me, I'd asked if he would find a way to put it in one of my walls. He'd smiled and said it was a beautiful poem, wasn't it? And then he'd said no, he couldn't use it for me, only one wall per poem, that was the rule. That was the magic. He'd find another one for me, he said. Somewhere. And he kissed the top of my head and turned over for sleep.

That was how he said it was over. Morning came, and as he was leaving to go to work, he turned to face me, pain in his eyes, and I said, "I know."

Someone told me recently that he's with a woman he just got engaged to. At first I thought, *Boy, that was fast.* Then I remembered the many nights he hadn't come to my house toward the end because he was meeting with a "demanding client," and I thought, *Oh.*

"Cecilia?"

Marilyn is talking from the closet.

"Yes?"

"Is it California Closets who did this? It's so well organized!"

"No, actually my best friend, Penny, and I designed that closet, and I had a carpenter friend build it."

"Well, it's wonderful. My goodness. You'll have to give me his name. I love the little ironing board built into the wall. And the jewelry display cases on the wall, what a brilliant idea! I buy so much jewelry and then I never wear it because I forget about it!"

I show her the rest of the house, and she tells me what she thinks it will sell for and that she has a client right now whom she thinks will be perfect for it. He's a very wealthy man getting a divorce, and he'll need some furniture—any chance I'd want to sell some of mine?

I almost laugh out loud. I can't count the number of times I've said, "Once you've made up your mind to do a good and true thing, the universe will go out of its way to help you." I tell Marilyn I'll sell everything but my bedroom furniture, artwork, books, and quilts. I probably should sell some of my quilts; with the seven Penny's codicil provided me with after she died, I now have far more than I'll ever use. But I can't part with a single one of them; they are like children to me. How could I sell something made in a pattern called Amish Shadow, or Evening Star, or even Broken Dishes? As for the one of Penny's called a Friendship quilt, well.

"Think of what you want to charge per piece of furniture, and collectively," Marilyn says. I see her out the door and then I call for help moving my bedroom furniture and clothes and the few other things that will be enough for now. When I dial the house's number, it's Renie who answers. "I'm ready," I say. I guess it's true.

RENIE BACKS HER TRUCK UP IN MY DRIVEWAY CROOKEDLY ENOUGH
that she takes a few lilac branches with her. The blossoms have gone
by now, thank goodness. "Sorry!" she yells, as she comes up the front
porch steps.

"No problem. Come in."

She crosses the threshold and stops dead in the living room.
"Whoa! You'll never fit all this stuff into our house."

"I'm not bringing most of it."

She runs her hand along the top of the antique Parisian gaming
table I bought a few years ago. "Why not?"

"I'm selling it. I'm selling just about everything."

She looks around the room. "How much for the chaise lounge?"

"You want it? You can have it."

"For how much?"

"For helping me move."

She goes and stretches out on it, puts her hands behind her head.
"Deal."

"I'm just taking my bedroom furniture and a few boxes of miscella-
neous stuff," I tell her. "I don't think any of it will be too heavy for us."

"Won't be too heavy for *me*," Renie says. "And if we need help,
we'll ask Riley."

"You brought the dog?" *Bad idea,* I think.

"He wanted to come. I told him he could come if he behaved. He will."

She stands, looks around again. "Wow. You're leaving a lot behind. Are you sure you aren't going to regret this?"

"You must have left a lot behind when you moved in."

"I didn't *have* much."

"I'm bringing the things that really matter to me. The rest . . . I don't know, I guess I've gotten to a point in my life where it's time to start shedding. And I'll tell you something: I've never regretted doing anything in my life as much as I've regretted *not* doing it. There were a few times when in my heart I knew the right thing to do, but I listened to other people, or I didn't have the guts, or it didn't make *sense*, or I don't know. . . . There was some false voice inside posing as logic when it was really just my own fear talking. The times I didn't stay true, didn't stay congruent, I paid the price."

"Yeah, well . . . That's hard to do, sometimes," Renie says.

She follows me upstairs and we take the mattress off my stripped bed and carry it down to the truck. Riley's in the cab of the truck, his head out the window, his tail wagging madly.

AFTER MY THINGS ARE moved into the house, I put fresh sheets and the Friendship quilt on my bed, then spend a couple of hours placing things where I think they should go. I put my desk in front of the window that looks out onto the backyard, and I sit there for a while, imagining the contours I could create for the garden, the bluestone chip paths, the location of the birdbath I'd like to have. For one minute, the memory of my old garden grabs hold, and I get a rush of fear thinking that I actually did this; there's no going back.

I jump when I hear a knock on the door, then go to open it.

Lise is standing there with a bouquet of apricot-colored roses in a green vase. "I just wanted to say welcome," she says.

"Thank you!"

She looks around the room. "It looks really nice in here, already. A lot different than when Sandy lived here. Then, you couldn't see the floor for the clothes all over it. And she covered the walls with pages ripped out of magazines. Floor to ceiling. It was interesting, I'll give her that. But this . . . this is really pretty. I love that quilt on your bed. Vintage, right?"

"At least one hundred years old. I can't resist old quilts. I've got a bunch of them."

She looks at her watch. "I've got to make some pre-op phone calls to a couple of my patients who are having surgery tomorrow. You'd be surprised how much people forget about what they were told. Or how they misinterpret what's in the handouts. Nerves, you know."

"I'd be the same way."

"Me, too. So I like to call, settle them down a bit, let them know that someone's in this with them, at least to the extent I can be. I'll see you at dinner." She leans forward, lowers her voice. "Renie's cooking, so don't expect a Joni meal."

She goes to her room, which is at the front of the house, over the porch, and closes the door. I put the flowers on my desk, loosen the arrangement, cross my arms, and stand back to regard it. The roses are lovely, just opening; they'll last for a long while. I still have books and clothes to unpack, but I'll do it later. For now, I'll go down and see if Renie needs any help.

When I start down the hall, I hear Lise on the phone. She's angry, shouting. "Well, I'm sorry that I bothered you. I haven't heard from you for a while and so I thought I'd check in. I won't keep you."

Silence.

I'm pretty sure that wasn't one of Lise's patients. I'm pretty sure that was her daughter.

I move quietly past and go downstairs and into the kitchen.

It's a mess—bowls and measuring cups and spoons out, bags of groceries half unpacked, onion peels on the floor.

"Can I help?" I ask Renie.

She looks up. "What are *you* going to do?"

"Well, I can peel. Chop. Dice."

"Really! Can you baste and blend?"

"Baste and *blend*? I can sauté and puree. I can flambé, toss, and skewer!"

Renie pulls a head of lettuce from the grocery bag, hands it to me. "How about broast? Can you broast?"

"Broasted lettuce?"

She shrugs. "I actually don't even know what 'broasted' means."

"I'm a little vague on that myself."

"Make a salad," she says. "And pour us both a glass of wine. There's some Chardonnay left over from last night in the fridge. God, I hate to cook."

I pour us glasses of wine, then move to the sink and start washing lettuce leaves. "I'm not crazy about it, either."

"Well, get used to it—we all have to take turns making dinner. It's one of Lise's rules of the house. Got to have a homemade meal for dinner. Got to keep the bathrooms clean, and there are no dishes allowed in the sink. No cutting things out of the newspaper until everyone's read it. If you take something from the first aid kit, replace it."

"You have a first aid kit?"

"A *major* first aid kit. There's stuff in there to start IVs! That's what happens when you live with a doctor. It's in the last bottom cupboard on the left. Oh, and here's a really important rule: No men can stay over. Or women, in my case."

"Really. Why can't anyone stay over?"

"Well, do the math. Could get crowded. But mostly Lise had a bad experience with one woman who lived here and had her boyfriend over all the time. He practically lived here. So she just made a hard-and-fast rule. It's a little fascist, but it works. Most people have their own place that we can go to. Here, wash these two carrots."

"You want them peeled, too?"

"We don't peel."

"You don't peel?"

"What is this, *Seinfeld?* No, we don't peel. Hardly ever. Too many nutrients in the peel, Lise says."

"What are we having besides salad?"

"Spaghetti and marinara sauce."

I wash the carrots, then ask if I should slice them.

"One sliced for the salad. One shredded, for the sauce."

I turn around. "Carrot in marinara sauce?"

"Yeah. It sweetens it."

"Really? I didn't know that."

We work companionably in the kitchen, Renie and I, and I have a sudden memory of working this way with Penny and Brice. To move myself away from that, I ask Renie what questions she answered in her advice column today.

"Oh, I had one that just made me nuts. This woman writes in that her mother-in-law criticizes her all the time. All the time, in front of her husband, and her husband never defends her. So I told her to take her mother-in-law out to lunch and give her a taste of her own medicine. I gave her a little list of things she might say. *Interesting outfit you're wearing; do you like that color against your face? Do you really want to sit facing out? Are you sure you want to order that? A spoon might work better for that. You put salt on that? Could you lower your voice a bit? I'm right here. Is that . . . is that lettuce in your teeth?* You know. And then I amped it up a bit for the big finish, where she points a fork at the mother-in-law's chest and says, *Listen. Whatever you think of me or what I'm doing, I don't want or need or expect any longer to hear. You managed to raise a spineless son by being judge and jury of everything, but I've got a long line of vertebrae running down my back and I'm going to tell you what he should have said a long time ago: Back off and butt out.*"

"Well," I say. "That ought to do it."

"Taste this," Renie says, holding out a spoon with salad dressing she just made.

"Wow," I say.

"Good?"

"*In*teresting!"

She stands there. Then she says, "Well. It won't kill us."

That night, just after we've finished eating, there's a phone call for me. Marilyn Watson got a full-price cash offer on my house from the man who just got divorced and he wants everything. All the furniture. The dishes and pots and pans. The garden hose, the mop and broom, the cans of soup in the cupboard, *everything*. "I think he just wants the thing to be over with," Marilyn says. "So tell me a day when you want to come over and get your personal things, and we'll be all set."

When I hang up the phone, I turn to my new roommates and dust off my hands. "Sold the house."

"*Already?*" Lise says.

"Yeah, he'd been ready to buy for a while, just needed the right house. And he wants everything in it, too!"

"Boy, are you lucky," Joni says.

I look into her friendly, open face and tell her I know I am. But a few minutes later, I go up into my room, close the door, and sit on my bed, my hands clasped in my lap, and in my chest is a raggedy sadness. Outside, the sun hangs at the horizon, then drops. Day is done.

'M LYING AWAKE, THINKING ABOUT DENNIS. IT'S BEEN OVER A week and no word from him. I wonder if he just wanted to say he was thinking of me and that's all. If on a languid day or a sleepless night he was flipping through memories and chanced upon me. I wish I'd kept a copy of the letter I sent him. Was it too much? Did it offend him somehow?

I turn on my side, flip my pillow, but it's no use; I'm wide awake. I went to sleep early, at nine o'clock, exhausted from having started work in the garden, and fell asleep right away. Then I woke up an hour later.

I should know better; I'm a creature of habit. I like to go to bed at eleven and get up at seven; everything works better that way.

I turn on the light and consider going downstairs, where someone is watching television, a movie, it sounds like. But I don't want to watch television, I want to go out onto the front porch and sit.

I put a robe on and go downstairs. It's Lise watching television, and when she sees me, she looks up and smiles. I point to the porch, then go out there.

I'm lying in the hammock swinging gently back and forth when Lise comes out. She has two cups of tea, and she hands me one. I like how Lise makes tea: no bags for her; she uses real tea leaves.

We sit in silence for a while, and finally I say, "Well, I think I made an ass of myself."

"Why do you say that?"

I tell her about hearing from Dennis, about the letter I wrote to him, how I've heard nothing back.

"But you've moved!" she says. "And the mail is so slow. He probably wrote you and you just haven't gotten it yet."

"Still, if he were really interested, don't you think he'd call?"

Lise shrugs. "From the way you described him, maybe not."

"I'm going to ask," I say, suddenly.

"What?"

"I'll be right back." I go up and get my wooden box from my closet. I bring it out onto the porch, put it on the wicker table, and open it. I light the black pillar candle that's in there, and take out my favorite deck of cards.

"What's all this?" Lise says, looking into the box. "Oh, the *I Ching*," she says. "I've heard about that. What else have you got in there?"

I show her and she pulls her chair up to the table. "Well, get busy asking," she says. "And when you're done, I've got a question, too."

Funny how drawn people are to the notion of fortune-telling, how susceptible they are to the thought of something supernatural offering a deeply personal revelation. The most pragmatic, the most sophisticated women used to fawn all over Cosmina, wanting her to tell them things they couldn't hear any other way.

I teach Lise how to make certain spreads with the cards, how to draw the Runes from the bag and place them out before her. I tell her how to throw the coins for the *I Ching*, how to record the straight and broken lines. She won't tell me her question, but she's not satisfied with any of the answers she gets; I can see the disappointment in her face. "Maybe you should read for me," she says.

"How about your tea leaves?"

"Can you do that?"

I shrug. "I don't know. Finish your tea and let me try."

Lise finishes her tea and hands me her cup. I tip it to the side and stare, just like Cosmina used to do. Well, there they are. Tea leaves.

I look up at Lise.

"What?" she says. Her face is serious in the candlelight, wanting.

I look down into the cup again, at the tea leaves. Most of them are grouped together, but there are a few apart, migrated up the sides of the cup.

"There has been a division," I say. "A separation."

Lise says nothing, but she leans in closer, so I know I'm on the right track. "But what has pulled apart is not really apart; it is made of what it separated from."

I don't look at her, fearful of her saying, "Oh, I see. Did you hear me yelling at Sandy?"

But she says nothing. She just sits. Waits. I tip the cup more, and some of the tea leaves that have separated join the larger mass. "A movement, a change of position, and things come together again." I look up at her. "Faith."

She starts to say something, but then the screen door bangs open and Renie and Joni come out. They're in their pajamas: Joni in a white nightgown, Renie in sweatpants and a T-shirt.

"What are you doing?" Renie asks.

I point to the box. "Telling fortunes."

Joni pulls a chair up. "Oh, boy. Can I play?"

I take a little offense at the term, but at its heart, I suppose we are playing.

Renie looks into the box and snorts. "Wait, let me put a sign in the window," she says. "SPECIAL: PALM READINGS, FIVE DOLLARS. How many of the words should I misspell?"

But she sits down. Eventually, she, too, has a question, though she won't tell us what it is. "Pull a card for me, Cece," she says.

"You should pull your own," I tell her and she says no, I should do it. I spread the cards and offer them to her.

"*You* do it," she says, and so I pull one out and give it to her. I hand her the book so that she can read the interpretation. She reads it to herself. Then she throws the book onto the table. "What a bunch of crap," she says, and goes inside.

The rest of us look at each other, and then I pick up the book and read aloud. "It says it's time for her to nurture herself or another," I say, and Joni says, "Oh, right. Nurture. That's Renie, all right. All *sweetums* and *nookums.*"

I read more bits and pieces: "*If you refuse to be cared for, it may be time for you to admit that you are human and in need of such care. If you are lonely, consider meeting with someone who means a great deal to you. . . . If you have been ignoring how you truly feel, if you have lost your deepest connection to yourself, it is time for a reunion.*"

"Yeah, lonely or alone, that's Renie," Lise says. Then she looks at me and says, "Oh!"

"What?" I say.

"You pulled the card," Lise says. "That message is for you. *Reunion.* Go and see him!"

"Go and see who?" Joni asks.

ONCE AGAIN, THERE IS NOTHING IN THE MAILBOX FROM DENNIS. I check my email again just in case he might have called my publisher to get the address, though why would he have done that when he has my cell number?

There is no email from him. Of course there isn't.

There is, however, an email from Alice Green. She's my lecture agent, and I love her. She takes great pleasure in doing her job, and she does it well. With her, I never have to worry about a thing: the travel arrangements, getting feedback from the people to whom I've presented a program, being paid promptly. The venues she finds for me are almost without exception really good. But I emailed her yesterday, telling her to not book any more events for me, that I'd let her know when I was ready to accept engagements again. Now she's asking me to call her, and so I do.

"You're *okay*, right?" she says.

"I'm fine," I say. "Really. I'm making some changes to my life. Pretty radical ones. I sold my house and practically everything in it and moved in with some other people. I'm taking some time off. I think I might want to work a lot less, maybe stop altogether. I want to do some traveling, some volunteering . . ."

"You know," she says. "I had a friend who sort of did what you're doing. She just up and left her life, really. Quit her job, sold her house, moved to a much smaller place. She said she wanted to be a citizen of the world, travel all over, not have to worry about taking care of anything. But after eight months, she was miserable. Because what she'd found out was that she loved taking care of things. And she loved her house. She hadn't realized how noisy or intrusive living in an apartment could be. She even tried to buy her house back, but she couldn't. So she bought another one, just down the block from her old one."

"Scary story."

"Well, right. I shouldn't have told you."

"No, I'm glad you did. I know you only told me out of concern. But listen: I love where I'm living. It's not a life I would have predicted for myself, but I love it! If things end up not working out after all, I'll move again. But for now, it's perfect.

"And about the house . . . I loved my house, too. But the other night I drove over and walked around my old neighborhood and looked at the lights on in my old place and I didn't feel any regret at all. And all the things that I could see from the sidewalk that he had rearranged . . . they just looked nice in there. I wished the guy who bought all that stuff well.

"When I got back to my new house, everybody was making ice cream sundaes in the kitchen and I just felt . . . glad. And here's something else: it wasn't a sudden decision, really; it had been brewing for a while. It took my doing it to understand how long I'd been *wanting* to do it, if you know what I mean."

"Hmmm," Alice says. "Now you've got *me* thinking!"

We laugh, and she says, "Let me know when you want to come back. I'll bet you could craft a great lecture about the very thing you're doing."

I thank her, and then call my editor. This will be a harder call, I think. But when I do speak with Celeste and tell her I'm taking a break from writing, she says, "Good for you. It's about time."

"Really?"

"Really. I'm so glad you're doing this, Cecilia. I feel you've needed it for some time."

"But . . ." I laugh, flustered. "I guess I thought you'd be disappointed. You know, good old reliable Cecilia, turning in her manuscripts year after year."

"Of course I love publishing you. But I care more about you than about your books. To be honest, I've felt a kind of sadness in you, and I was beginning to get worried."

"A sadness? Well, as you know, my best friend died."

"Yes, and again I'm sorry for that. But I think all this began before that. You haven't taken a break for . . . well, for as long as I've known you."

"Huh. That's what Penny told me, too. Before she got sick, she kept telling me to slow down."

"Maybe I should have told you the same thing. But listen, I want you to take all the time you need. You know all of us here love you and wish you the best."

After I hang up, I go to the website for the Arms. I click on Volunteering and look at the various possibilities. I don't know exactly what I'm interested in doing, and the photos of the patients make me a little nervous. But I'll go for an interview and find something I can do. I promised.

And speaking of promises, after the garden is in, maybe I'll travel a bit. I'll go on a road trip. And maybe I'll just drop in on Dennis when I do. Surprise.

Or maybe that's not a good idea.

I close my eyes.

What have you got to lose?

"Pride."

What good has that ever brought you?

"What if it's clear that he doesn't want to see me? And I will have come all that way!"

Then you will get back in your car and see what else there is to see.

I look out the window into the clear blue sky. Here comes the drone of an airplane, the sound of a jogger running by. Here I am in the world, free.

I go outside and get in my car, planning to take a ride over to Summit Avenue, to see what the Arms looks like. But halfway there, I turn around. Not yet.

IN THE KITCHEN, JONI IS MASSAGING CHICKEN BREASTS. SHE USES a big heavy mallet but she doesn't pound; she moves the smooth side of the tool across the meat like she's ironing it. Her hair, that explosion of long golden curls, is corralled by a green-and-white bandanna.

"Chicken schnitzel," Joni tells me, before I can ask.

"Still no letter," I say, sliding into the booth.

"Maybe he's taking his time, thinking of what to say." Then, looking up, her blue eyes bright, she says, "You don't think he's on the way here, do you? You sent him that postcard with your new address, right? What if he just shows up?"

It's not impossible that he would spontaneously appear, but I doubt it, and I tell her this.

"He might also be really busy with something," she says. "Don't take it personally."

"Oh well," I say, sounding more dejected than I mean to.

"Why don't *you* go *there* and surprise him?"

"You know, I was just thinking of that. I want to take a road trip, anyway. And then I could sort of drop in on him. I'm really curious to see what he's like now!"

Joni reaches for two eggs, cracks them at the same time, then starts beating them. "It's so powerful, old flames. I once found a treasure trove of letters from a guy who was one of my boyfriends in high school, letters he'd written to me the first year I was in college. They were in a suitcase I kept doll clothes in when I was a little girl. I found it in the basement one day and brought it up, thinking I'd clean it out and give it to my daughter for her dolls. But when I opened it up, there were all these letters. I'd forgotten I'd put them in there.

"I brought them into the bedroom and sat on the bed to read a couple, and I ended up reading all of them. I remember it was a rainy day, lots of thunder, and I had the bedside light on and I was wearing a lilac-colored cardigan that had a hole in one elbow and I had an apron on over that—I'd just finished braiding egg bread and I was letting it rise—but I read those letters and time just fell away. I was back there with Pete Massotti, state wrestling champ. I was at Guffy's Drive-in, sharing French fries with him; lying in the backseat of his car and making out with him; getting all dressed up to go to the prom with him and wondering if I should go all the way that night—which I did not—and, sweet boy that he was, he didn't pressure me. When Erin came home from school, when the front door banged open, I looked up from one of those letters and it was like I was coming out from under anesthesia.

"I came downstairs, and Erin, she was seven then, said, 'What *happened?*' And I . . . I just didn't know what to say. She stood there, staring at me. I must have looked like some kind of zombie. She asked if she could go next door and I said yes and then I went to check on the bread and it had over-risen but I put it in the oven anyway and then I went back upstairs and gathered up all those letters that were spread out on the bed and I . . . Oh God, I threw them away. Isn't that awful? I threw them away. I wish I hadn't done that. But they were so powerful, they scared me. I loved my husband, I was so happy with him, but I swear, if Pete had shown up right after I read those letters,

I might have run away with him. In my apron and my sweater with a hole in it."

She rolls a lemon on the counter to soften it, cradles it in her hand to sniff it, rolls it some more. I love watching Joni in the kitchen. For her, cooking is a practical sacrament. At work, she makes things whose names I can't pronounce and wouldn't know even if I could pronounce them. She showed me Ultramarine's menu for the season and I told her it should come with a glossary. But here at home she makes simpler food, healthy comfort food, and it's always delicious.

"Don't you wish you could see him again?" I ask.

"Who? Pete?"

"Yeah."

She shrugs. "I don't know. Maybe. But I think maybe it was just one of those times when a memory picks you up and carries you off like dandelion fluff. I'll tell you what I would like to do. I'd like to go on that road trip with you. That would be fun; I love road trips."

"Come with me!"

She laughs. "I can't leave work. I can never leave work! I'll probably die at work. But you should go, definitely. Look, he contacted you first!"

"True. Do you want some help cooking? Got anything easy I could do?"

"You want to frost the cake?"

"We're having cake?"

"Yeah, chocolate cake and cream cheese frosting. It's a healthier version: whole wheat pastry flour, buttermilk, canola oil, brown sugar. The frosting isn't so healthy, but it's a birthday cake; you have to let up a little when it's a birthday cake."

"Whose birthday?"

"I picked this day to be Renie's birthday. You have to surprise her; she says she doesn't like you to make a fuss over her birthday, but she kind of does like it. So what we do is pick a random day every year, and voilà."

"I didn't know; I didn't get her anything."

"She doesn't like presents. She really doesn't, that part's true. One of us always gets her a joke present, though; Lise is doing it this time. We do sing the birthday song and light the candles. You've got to sing the birthday song and light the candles, no matter what age you are. On my dad's last birthday, we put eighty candles on the cake, and it melted all the frosting!" She dips a chicken breast into the flour, then into the egg, tenderly. It looks like a mother bathing her newborn.

"So where is the cake?"

"On the back porch, cooling. It should be ready to frost by now."

I go outside to get it, put it on the kitchen table. It's beautiful, nearly black, and it smells so good. "Where's the frosting?"

"Not made yet. You can make it. Stick of butter, cake of cream cheese, a little salt, a little vanilla, powdered sugar; nothing to it."

"How much vanilla? And salt? And powdered sugar?"

She stares at me, her hands on her hips. Then she says, "Okay, I'll make it; you frost it."

"Good idea." I sit at the table and watch as Joni finishes preparing the chicken breasts.

"Did you always like to cook?" I ask.

"Oh, yeah. Always. My mom was really great about letting me help. I think part of the reason is that she really didn't like cooking; it was a relief for her to hand it off. So as soon as I was able, I began making dinner for the family. I loved it. I really did. I still remember the first meal I ever made: tomato soup and toasted cheese sand-wiches.

"Every day, I would come home from school and put on my yellow apron and forget all about April Hastings and Beverly Whitman. They were awful. They made my my life hell all four years of high school. One day they sat behind me on the bus and put *gum* in my hair, and it took my mom forever to get it out.

"But anyway, I found cooking to be relaxing. I still do, at least when I cook here. The restaurant is another thing." She looks up from unwrapping the cake of cream cheese. "Honestly? I've never said this out loud, but sometimes I wonder how much longer I can take it."

"Maybe we should ask the cards."

She smiles. "Maybe we should."

AT DINNER, I ANNOUNCE that I'm going to take a road trip. To see Dennis Halsinger. And that I'm pretty nervous about it.

"How did you meet him, anyway?" Joni asks.

I laugh. "You know how I met him? I met him because of a loaf of bread."

"That's a pretty good first line for a how-I-met-him story," Renie says.

"I guess it is."

"So . . . what about the bread?" Lise asks.

"You want to hear the story?" I ask, and they all three nod.

"Well, I was nineteen and living in my first apartment. It was this tiny studio apartment at the back of a house near the university, and the act of buying a whole loaf of bread seemed like a minor miracle."

"I remember that feeling," Joni says. "I used to get excited that I could pick out whatever Kleenex box I wanted. And that I could eat the same thing three nights in a row if I wanted."

"You cooked in your first apartment?" Renie asks.

"Of course. Didn't you?"

"No. What was in my refrigerator in my first apartment was cheap beer. And I kept my underwear in there, when it was hot out."

"But what about the bread?" Joni says.

"Okay, so I'd been to the little grocery store not far from me, and I was walking past Dennis's house when he came out the door and smiled at me. I stopped dead in my tracks and said, 'You want some bread?'"

"Why?" Lise says.

"Why did I ask him that?"

"Yeah."

"I'll bet he was handsome," Joni says.

"He was really handsome. He was tall and well built and he had long blond hair and these blue eyes with a kind of far calm like a lot of hippies did back then. He was wearing bell-bottom jeans and a white cable-knit sweater and he just . . . he just . . ."

"Oh my God, you jumped his bones, right?" Renie says. "You were all about free love in those days, right?"

"We were, but I was still a virgin. I didn't really want to be. I think if he'd asked me that day, I would have gone right to bed with him."

"Different times," Lise says.

"Different times," I agree. "But anyway, when I offered him the bread, he said sure and he invited me into his house and we sat at his table and ate it. And you'll appreciate this, Joni: he had homemade apple butter that we put on it."

"He made apple butter?"

"No, his mother did. And it had the prettiest handmade label, a trio of apple trees, done in watercolors. I told him how much I liked the apple butter and he went to the cupboard and got a full jar and put it in my grocery bag. And then he said he had to run some errands, did I want a ride home, and I told him no, that I lived really close by and I told him where. Then he went outside and he climbed into his powder-blue Chevy stepside, and I—"

"I love those trucks!" Renie says.

"Well, I do, too, and when I saw that he drove one—"

"But when did you sleep with him?" Joni asks.

"Oh. Well. That was later. But something else really wonderful happened first. The morning after I met him, I came outside, and Dennis was standing in my backyard. He asked if I wanted to go with him to the March on Washington. And I said no."

"You said *no*?" Renie asks, incredulous. "To the March on Washington? The 'sixty-nine moratorium to end the war in Vietnam?"

"I said no."

"Over two hundred and fifty thousand people went to that march!" Renie says. "It was the largest antiwar protest in history!"

"I know," I say.

I'm still embarrassed about not having gone. I had no good reason not to. If I'd gone, I would have earned an internal merit badge. I would have felt something, understood something, committed far earlier than I eventually did to my antiwar stance. I would have taken my part as a citizen of the world, I would have seen that I *was* a citizen of the world, a small part of an organic whole. But a vital part.

I might as well make a full confession. "Guess what else I said no to. Woodstock."

"No!" Renie says.

"I would have said no to Woodstock, too," Lise says.

"Not me," Joni says. "I remember wanting to go, but I was too young. I asked my parents and they said no and then for a whole day I made plans with my friend Betsy Schuler to hitchhike there but we got too scared to do it. But why didn't you go?"

I smile. "You know why? When some friends came to get me for a last-minute pilgrimage they were making, I said, 'Isn't it raining there?' "

The women laugh, but then it's quiet, and I'd guess we're all thinking about lost opportunities, great regrets.

"But Dennis . . ." Lise says.

"Oh. Right. So I said no to the march, where he was going the next day. But that evening, I came back from having seen a movie and I found a note on the table. Dennis had been there earlier; my room-mate had let him in before she went off to spend the night with her boyfriend. The note said just three words: *Cecilia. Tonight. Dennis.*"

"Oh, I love it," Joni says.

"Why?" Renie says, indignant. "It's so presumptuous!"

"It's *romantic*," the rest of us say, in unison.

Lise's cell rings and she holds up a hand. "Let me make sure it's not the answering service—I'm on call." She looks at the number, and her face hardens. "Not the service," she says. "Go ahead."

Her daughter? I think. But I go on with the story. "Okay. So . . . I read the note and I got ready. I bathed, put on clean clothes, brushed my hair. I waited a long time, and he didn't come. Finally I gave up and went to bed, but fully clothed, just in case he did show up. I re-member I put a record called 'One Stormy Night' on the stereo to fall asleep to, even though it was redundant; it was raining.

"I woke up to a knocking at the door. I answered and there was Dennis, and the night looked so big behind him. I had no idea what time it was. I opened the door for him to come in. But he gestured for me to come out, so I followed him around to the front of the house.

He had a motorcycle with him; I was surprised I hadn't heard it when he pulled up outside, but I hadn't. I got on the back and we went riding. It had stopped raining, but the streets were still wet. Dennis dipped really low from side to side, and it wasn't scary; it was like dancing. I rested my chin on his shoulder and looked at all the things we passed by and I watched his face in the side-view mirror and I kept thinking, *He is so handsome.*

"When he brought me home, I made us peppermint tea. We brought our mugs out to the back steps to watch the sun come up. The sky was all rose and apricot colors, and then it started turning blue, and the birds began to call. It felt like a privilege to be up at that hour. It was like church. We went inside and he lay in my bed next to me. Neither of us spoke. For a long time, we were still, letting ourselves get warm. Then he rose up on his elbow and looked down at me, and he gently stroked the hair off my forehead, then back from my temples. He kissed me once, a long, deep, and perfect kiss. And that was all we did. He lay down beside me and we didn't say another word until he had to go. That kept it like a dream. Joan Baez has a line in a song: *Speaking strictly for me, we both could have died then and there.* Whenever I hear it, I think of that time with Dennis."

I stop talking, realize I've told this latter part of the story without really being here; I've been elsewhere, lost in the reverie.

I look around the table, a little embarrassed.

Joni practically whispers, "But you didn't have sex that time?"

"You know, when I told my best friend, Penny, that story I just told you, she said, 'That was your first time.' And I said no, that came later. And she said, 'No, that was your first time.' And she was right. Dennis and I made an unalterable connection that night. It was the first time I'd met someone so fully in the middle. For me, it was a transcendent moment, something that superseded anything physical."

Joni says, "Whew! It's a good thing you decided to go and see him. Because otherwise I would have had to take you. And I don't have time to take you."

"He's your one," Lise says, quietly.

And I nod, thinking I know exactly what she means. What I felt for Dennis right from the start was a pull like gravitation, a feeling that I already knew him in my bones, and that thus far in my life I had only been piddling around, waiting to find him. I know how this sounds. But it's true as blue, as Dennis himself might say. Or would have, in those days.

"Your first," Lise says. "There's something so evocative about those words: *the first.*" She sits there for a minute, thinking, and then she says, "Where are you going, again?"

"Well, Dennis is in Cleveland, so I'm going there. But it's a road trip, so I'm perfectly willing to roam around and go almost anywhere else, too."

"Des Moines?"

"Sure. Why not?"

"Well, I might come, then. I just might."

"Who are you going to see?" Joni asks.

"If I go, I'll tell you," Lise says. Then, "So, Renie. What came in at work today?" Clearly she wants to change the subject.

Renie thinks for a moment, then says, "One from a woman whose son doesn't like her boyfriend. One from yet another Bridezilla . . . Oh, and one from someone whining that the person who gives her massages keeps doing it wrong."

Joni frowns. "Are you kidding?"

"I wish I were."

"So what are you going to tell her?"

"I haven't decided yet. But it will probably have something to do with suggesting she try hard manual labor rather than get massages."

"What will you tell the woman whose son doesn't like the boy-friend?"

"That's a hard one. The boyfriend is why she got divorced. So how can she expect the kid to like him?"

"The mother has a right to her life," Lise says.

"The kid has rights, too," Renie fires back.

Joni has left the table, but now she comes in carrying the birthday cake, candles ablaze. "Guess what, Renie?"

"Oh, is it my birthday today?"

Joni starts singing the birthday song, and the rest of us join in.

"I want a huge piece of cake," Renie says. "Do we have ice cream?"

"Frozen yogurt," Joni says. "I'll get it as soon as you open your gift."

Renie rolls her eyes and accepts the large, gaily wrapped present. She opens it and says, "Oh thank God, it's just what I needed." She holds up a makeup kit, something obviously designed for little girls, all pink rhinestoned pots and brushes and tiny lipstick tubes. " 'Just Like Mommy,' " she reads. She stares at it, then drops it. She puts her elbows on the table, her face in her hands, and begins to cry.

"Renie?" Joni says, and Lise, seated next to her, puts her arm around her.

"What's wrong?" Lise asks, gently, and Renie waves her hand: not now. After a moment, she puts her hands into her lap and says, "I have a daughter. Somewhere. When I was nineteen years old, I gave up a newborn baby. She's twenty now. She was born in Winona on May first at four-nineteen in the morning. Seven pounds, twelve ounces. Twenty and one-half inches. Very dark, thick hair that already was over the tops of her ears. Mouth like a tiny little rosebud. One dimple in the left cheek, just one.

"When I was in labor, I refused painkillers because I wanted to feel everything. That was all I could give her, was to be fully present at the time of her birth. It hurt a lot. I held her for seven minutes after they stitched me up and then I never saw her again. I named her Camille. It was a secret—I knew her adoptive parents had named her Haley, but I named her Camille. That's who *I'd* like to see. So. Let's have that cake."

THAT NIGHT, I TAKE RILEY out for a walk. He sniffs at the base of every tree trunk we pass and at various spots on the ground here and there for what seem to me to be unreasonable lengths of time, one paw held up high against his chest as though to lessen any possible contamination of the site with his own smell. Or perhaps it's the dog equivalent of a person reflexively putting her hand to her chest, which often happens when people see something particularly interesting: witness visitors at museums, leaning forward to look at a thousand-year-old artifact in a glass case.

We walk three blocks, then four. It's a nice temperature, the stars are out, and I want a little time to think. I wonder why I haven't felt any regret about stopping work. Did it mean so little to me?

There is a lot of satisfaction, a lot of joy, that can come from doing something you love and that you're good at, and I was good at my job. And yet it was nothing I ever expected to do.

In my late twenties, I took a job helping to care for a dying woman who was married to an extremely rich and powerful insurance magnate named Clement Burke. Every evening, he used to come and sit by his wife, and after she fell asleep for the night, he would talk to me until eleven o'clock, when it was time for me to go home. I was between jobs, casting about and beginning to feel a little desperate, looking for something that would stick. He was a man who had built his fortune on believing in things like *Positive Mental Attitude,* a man who, even in the face of his wife's incurable illness, would tell her every night, *Every day, in every way, you are getting better and better.* At first I thought it was cruel, but it seemed to comfort her; and finally I decided that getting better didn't necessarily mean getting cured, at least not to them. There was something that happened between the two of them when they said those words together, she lying pale in her blue nightie and holding on to his freckled hands, he with his face so close to hers and so full of love. There was something that happened that was beyond me, but that I understood anyway. It's like the way you can read scientific principles that may be beyond you intellectually, but that your poet's soul embraces.

After his wife died, Clem (as he asked me to call him) told me that he had very much appreciated the way I'd been able to rally his wife where others had failed. I got her to eat a bit, to get out of bed and sit by the window and look at the view, to allow a brief visit from this grandchild or that. Whenever she smiled, I felt a quick uptick inside myself: it felt good to provide her with whatever small pleasures I could.

Clem suggested that I become a motivational speaker, and that in fact he would be willing to hire me himself to do inspirational retreats with his sales force. At first it seemed a bizarre suggestion, but then the more I thought about it, the more I liked the idea—why not try to help others be their best selves, why not turn what seemed to be a natural proclivity into a good-paying profession? I'd get to travel a lot, too, which I'd never been able to do before; those retreats were held in beautiful and interesting places. One time it might be a secluded abbey surrounded by layers of lush green, where you could hear the Divine Office chanted at specified hours throughout the day. The next time might be at the Arizona Biltmore or in some pink towering structure in Miami so close to the beach the ocean seemed to be in your room with you. The job took me to Alaska and Hawaii, and more than once to luxury hotels abroad: London, Paris, Rome, Madrid. After I had worked for Clem for ten years, he died, and I didn't care to work for his son, who lacked the qualities that made me so admire his father. Using all I had learned about the tenderness and fragility and vagaries of the human spirit, the needs and frustrations that we all share, I started writing self-help books. Then I began doing speaking gigs as well, based on those books.

I worked because I needed to, of course, but I also worked because it was the way I communicated best. I had always had a shy love of people; they broke my heart a million times a day. But from the time I was a little kid, I was a loner. I never liked recess. My favorite teacher in elementary school let me stay in from it; I always wanted to stay in. It's not that I'm antisocial; it's that I care too much, and so I have a lot of fears. It takes a lot for me to really get close to someone in an honest and undefended way.

A couple of years ago, there was a day when I had a lot of work to do. But I ignored it and took the whole day off. I loved that day, the ease and deliberateness of it, the way it put me in touch with my species in a way that was not virtual. Instead of talking to an imaginary reader, I talked over the fence with my next-door neighbor about gardening. Later, I sat in the backyard and listened to the birds, watched the movement of the clouds and the progression of the line of shade that moved across the back deck. I put a CD on the stereo

and listened to it the way I used to listen to music: eyes closed, atten-
tive to the nuances in a song, the way that a tiny shift in volume or
diction or timing or chord structure could enlarge the feeling, the
meaning.

I went to a bookstore and browsed. I ended up buying Thomas
Hardy's *Tess of the d'Urbervilles*, because I'd never read it. I went to
a coffee shop and sat at a little table with my latte and read for an hour
and then I closed the book and engaged in conversation with anyone
who wanted to talk: a young woman with hair to her waist and wide
brown eyes who had just moved here; a man in a wheelchair with an
oxygen tank who made you forget his disability in the space of one
minute; a four-year-old boy who climbed up in the chair opposite me
and told me all about his toy truck while his grateful mother talked to
her girlfriend. Stepping away from my routine for just that one day
made me feel as if I'd taken a vacation to some idyllic place. But that
"place" was in me: a kind of rare peace and a deepened appreciation
for other people; the small kindnesses I witnessed, the way I
remembered—because we do forget—that we're all in this together.

But you know what usually happens when you take a vacation to a
place that galvanizes you and makes you feel like you're going to
change your life. You come home and get right back into your old
habits. Meanwhile, a slow fire burns.

A man comes down the sidewalk and for one breathless moment,
I think it's Dennis. It's not; the man passes and I see that in fact he
looks nothing at all like Dennis, or at least nothing like Dennis used
to look. Who knows what he looks like now? Is it possible he's bald,
with a paunch?

Anyway. Here I am. Free from my job, and not living alone anymore. Thus far, the only disadvantage I've found to living with others

is that you can't mandate noise levels. No one in the house is abusive with noise, but even the television turned on to a reasonable level can interfere when you're thinking. It's a small price to pay; I'm happy with my decision.

Last night I sat on the floor of Joni's bedroom with her, fancy cookbooks piled all over, helping her look for interesting appetizers she could adapt for use at Ultramarine. Those new cookbooks are all well and good, but the cookbooks she really likes are those from long ago. She buys them in antiques stores and at garage sales. She likes the notes the owners wrote in small, often perfect cursive: *Doug loved!* or *Used for Mary's 16th birthday* or *Add lemon jce—a bit too sweet.* Many of those old recipes she uses when she cooks for us. One we all love is the red cabbage with cloves and apple in it.

I like being in Joni's bedroom. It's messy but comfortable. She has an antique bed with an off-white wrought-iron frame, and I gave her one of my quilts to put on it, a double wedding ring in dusty roses and pale greens and ivory. There's a chandelier she bought on a trip to London, all curling leaves and flowers. She has a dresser that belonged to her grandmother, and on it are framed pictures of friends, relatives, and food: a blue plastic crate full of lemons, a platter piled high with pasta, a lattice-top pie nestled into a red-and-white-checked dish towel.

There is also a glass tray full of old perfume bottles, all empty; Joni doesn't wear perfume because it interferes with her tasting things, but she likes the evocative shapes of the bottles. I've already decided that for her birthday, which I know is the fourth of July, I'm going to get her the most elegant atomizer I can find.

Lise's room is as neat as Joni's is messy. Clean lines, colors of black and white and gray, no froufrou, just the way she dresses—I've never seen any jewelry but pearl studs on Lise. She has miniblinds, halogen lamps, that sort of thing.

I've yet to be invited into Renie's room. I have had a quick glance every now and then; she's got one wall full of books and CDs, and she has some Asian influence going on in there: black lacquer furniture, an orange-red silk duvet cover. And my old chaise lounge, which is neutral enough not to look out of place.

I turn around and start for home. I think we were all greatly surprised at what Renie revealed at dinner. She wouldn't say anything more about it then, but I want very much to talk to her, if she's willing. There's a story I could tell her.

When I get back to the house, I stand for a while on the sidewalk in front of it. Lights are on, the windows are deep yellow squares. I see Lise moving about inside. I know how the house will smell when I come in, I know where to hang Riley's leash and that I should check his water dish. I know that if my roommates are talking about something, they'll catch me up on whatever it is. I am comfortable here, I belong, I am home. When I was a little girl, I used to make a basket of my hands to hold a feeling of joy that came upon me, then flatten my hands against my chest, as if to make it part of me. Not understanding that it already was.

"WHERE'S RENIE?" I ASK, when I come into the living room.

Joni, watching something on television with Lise, points to the upstairs. I head up there, thinking I'll knock on Renie's door with a Penelope Lively novel that she saw me with and expressed interest in reading after I was done.

I get the book from my bedroom, knock on her door. "Renie?" I say softly, into the crack. I suppose it's possible that she's sleeping, early as it is.

But no. I hear, "What."

"I've got that book you wanted to read."

"Okay. I'll get it tomorrow."

"Do you mind if I come in?"

Nothing.

But then the door opens, and Renie says, "What do you want?"

"Would you like to talk?"

"About . . . ?"

"About what you said at dinner. About your daughter. I'd like to tell you something."

She sighs, puts a hand on her hip. Then she opens the door wider and I go in.

She's been working. Her laptop is on, the cursor flashing. She puts the lid down on it and gestures toward the chaise lounge. The walls are painted the most interesting color; it's nothing I could put a name to. Green? Gray? A strange shade of blue? There's a bedside lamp made with rice paper, a black lacquer bowl holding tiny scrolls of paper tied with red ribbon. I can sense Renie's nervousness as I look around, and so I sit down, push a pillow made from a Japanese fabric in colors of green, orange, and cream up against my middle. Thus defended, I start my story.

"When I was in college, I had a friend named Patty, who got pregnant by some guy who wanted nothing more to do with her when he found out she was carrying his child. He told her to get an abortion but not to expect him to pay for it."

If a nod can be bitter, Renie's is.

"She didn't want to get an abortion. She was pro-choice, and her choice was to go ahead and have the child and give it up for adoption. So she stayed in school and finished out the year, and then that summer she gave birth.

"We didn't care, her friends and I. I mean, we cared about her, but the idea of having a baby was so foreign to our lives at the time, we just . . . We didn't care. We felt bad for her that she got pregnant and had to go through all that, but what we figured was that she'd deliver the baby, give it up, and that would be that. Clean slate.

"I remember going to her apartment with another friend to see her, about two weeks after she delivered. And she was okay, she didn't seem particularly devastated, as we'd feared she might—look what had happened to her *body!*—but all she wanted to talk about was that baby, about having the baby, what it felt like to have that child in her arms. We didn't *care.* I think we both thought, *What's the big deal?* That baby is out of your life. Move on. Come on out with us tonight, we're going to the Triangle Bar to hear some music, come *on.*

"We lost touch with her soon afterward. Not because we stopped trying to see her, but because she didn't want to see us. It took a little growing up for me to understand why, but by then it was too late. I'm still haunted by the memory of her standing in her kitchen, trying to tell us what had happened to her, what she'd had and what she'd lost. Trying to tell us that it was not over for her, it would never be over."

Renie is staring into her lap; I can't tell what her expression is.

"So . . . I don't know. I just wanted to tell you that. I don't have children, I haven't been pregnant, but I think I understand, at least a lot more than I used to, what it might be like for you to have had to carry this. And I don't know if you were serious about trying to see her, but maybe you should."

"I don't know where she is."

"I'll bet you could find her."

"Yeah, maybe." She looks up. "I have some work to do."

I stand. "Okay."

"But thanks, Cece. Really."

"Sure."

I go back downstairs and sit on the sofa. A commercial comes on, and Joni gets up. "I'm getting more water. Anyone want anything?" Then, quietly, "Is she okay?"

I nod. Then I sit down and watch the black-and-white movie, where a man is pinning a corsage onto a woman wearing a dress that looks like it's made of crushed stars. After he does, the couple look deeply into each other's eyes.

Joni sighs loudly.

"I agree," Lise says. "All the blatant sex these days isn't sexy at all. Give me a guy pinning a corsage onto my shoulder just above my breast, and then lingering there just for a moment."

"Give me a guy brushing my hand," I say.

Joni says, "Give me a guy who lights two cigarettes and hands me one." She thinks for a minute, then says, "Wait. Never mind. That would make me burst out laughing. Plus I don't smoke."

I'M SOUND ASLEEP when I'm awakened by a kind of bumping at my bedroom door. I open it, expecting to find Riley, feeling a little smug that he now sometimes wants to spend his nights with me rather than Lise, but it's Renie, standing there. "Sorry to wake you up. Can I come in?"

"Of course," I say and step aside. She comes in and does a slow turn around, taking in the Friendship quilt on the bed, the huge desk, the pillows I've put on the window seat, the blue velvet club chairs sitting on either side of a round table. I point to one of the chairs, and she sits down. I sit opposite her.

"Your room turned out nice," she says, speaking quietly, nearly whispering.

"Thanks," I whisper back.

"It's really late."

"That's okay."

Renie takes in a breath, clasps her hands together. "So, I just wanted to tell you something about . . . about Camille, how she happened."

I nod.

"Did you ever read Stendhal? *Memoirs of an Egotist*?"

I must look puzzled, because she adds, "French writer, someone more interested in people's insides than in their outsides; you'd probably love him. He said, *It only needs a small quantity of hope to beget love.* And he is said to have made an ass of himself in love. He was apparently besotted by a woman who was really beautiful and charismatic. She was also some general's wife. Stendhal followed her all over the place, sometimes wearing disguises. He'd try to get invited to parties where she was going to be. You'd think she'd have had him arrested or at least told him to shove off, but no. She let him come and see her, but only twice a month. He would come and sit in her parlor and die of longing. That anguish is said to have contributed to his art.

"My story is I also fell in love with a woman who was pretty much unobtainable. Her name was Sharon Hart. She let me hang around her, though, she let me hang around her a lot, she *asked* me to hang around with her. I felt like she was gay but not quite out. She dated so many guys, she went through them like Kleenex, but she flirted with me big-time. She'd touch my hand, or my hair, she'd lean in overly close to tell me something in a noisy place. Once she brushed a crumb off my face, and she took way too long to do it.

"There was a time when we went camping together, and a thunderstorm came late at night. We were in our tent, side by side in sleeping bags, and there was this really loud crack of thunder. She let out a little yelp and grabbed me. I thought it was an excuse, you know, and I . . . Well, I tried to kiss her. But she pushed me away, and then she apologized. And rather than giving up on her, I thought the fact that she apologized meant she just wasn't ready. So I continued to hang out with her, I continued to love her and hope that soon she'd be able to admit to a sexual orientation that seemed obvious to me.

"But then she began dating this jock, Ed Michaels, big football jock. She began spending more and more time with him and it just drove me nuts. Ed liked me. We were in Introduction to Sociology together, and he thought I was really funny and smart. He didn't know I was gay, and I didn't tell him, I let him flirt with me. But then when Sharon started getting closer to him, I thought, *Okay. Watch this,* and I went over to Ed's apartment one night and got drunk with him and then went to bed with him. It wasn't easy for me to do that. He was the only man I'd ever been with and the feel of his body was just abhorrent to me, especially his . . ."

We both smile.

"Anyway, I wanted to show her that he was no prize; that he would betray her, just like that. She got the message and she broke up with him. And I got pregnant. What need had I for birth control? Ed said he'd pull out and he did, but . . .

"Anyway. Not only did Sharon break up with Ed but she broke up with me. I lost her. Then I lost the baby, I gave her up, and I never wanted to think about that kid again. Never wanted to think about any of it. Only . . . I do think about it. A lot. Especially in May."

She looks up at me. "You know, I have an eight-year-old niece named Madeline who likes to write stories. She wrote one about herself and her friend Lucy and how they were offered a ride in 'Mr. Excellent's Flying Machine.' Lucy was afraid to get in but Madeline did, and she got to fly to the moon. She ends the story by saying, 'I got in and Lucy didn't and now little birds are pecking at her heart.' Ever since I gave my baby up, little birds have pecked at my heart. So when I got that dumb makeup kit for a birthday present . . ."

She sighs. "I never told anyone the whole story."

"I'm glad you told me."

"I don't know if I am or not. But as long as I'm at it, you want to know something else?"

"Sure."

"I know where she is."

"Who?"

"Camille. Haley."

I lean forward in my chair. "Where?"

Renie smiles. "Winona, Minnesota. She never left. I found her current address. I Googled the place where she lives. It's an apartment building right near Winona State. I would guess she's a student there."

"So . . . do you think you should contact her?"

"When you came to my room, I was writing her a letter."

"Really?"

"I don't know if I'll send it. I just wanted to get some things off my chest. But maybe I will finish writing it." She stands. "Thanks for listening."

"Thanks for telling me."

"Don't tell the others I found her."

"I won't."

"For now, I'll just say I'm going on the trip with you. Then we'll see what happens."

"What's her last name?" I ask.

"Redmund. Haley Redmund."

Hearing Haley's name makes her suddenly so much realer to me. I see her as a long-haired, straight-mouthed girl, cautious in her dealings with strangers. I go over to Renie and hug her. She's stiff as an ironing board, but she stands still and takes it.

"Good night," she says, pulling away.

"Good night."

She closes my door softly, and I go back to bed, but I can't sleep. In the refrigerator is that cake. I put on my robe, tiptoe down the hall. As I pass Renie's door, she opens it. "I forgot to get the Lively book from you," she whispers. And then, "Where are *you* going?"

"Cake."

"Right behind you," she says.

THE NEXT MORNING, I GET A CALL FROM THE ARMS, ASKING IF I can come for an interview. It occurs to me to tell them I'm going away—I'm going to take that road trip no matter what—but I might as well get the interview over with. I have enough time to visit my mother on the way; I'll stop by Cecil's bakery for her.

When I get to my mother's apartment, I knock on the door three times before she answers. And then she only cracks the door. She's dressed in her robe but fully made up. "Are you going out?" I hold up the bakery bag. "Look what I got you."

"Oh, sweetheart, not right now."

"They're those apricot pastries you like so much." I start to come in, but she blocks me.

"I really have to finish getting ready."

From the back of the apartment, I hear someone sneeze. It's a man sneeze.

We stare at each other.

"Okay, well, I'll just be going then," I say. I start down the hall.

"Cecilia?"

I turn around reluctantly.

"Leave the pastry?"

I give her the bag, then start down the hall again.

"Thank you!" she calls after me, and I hold up my hand, *You're welcome.*

I get into the car and sit there for a minute, then start it. Guess I'd better start calling ahead.

Ten minutes later, I'm parked in front of the Arms. It's one of the smaller mansions on Summit, but it's lovely. I sit looking at it for a while, wondering what people think about when they first come here to stay, knowing it's very likely the last place they'll be. I imagine that mixed in with the sadness there might be great relief. I hadn't known that Penny had come to look at this place. By then, the person she confided in most was Brice. "Penny," I say softly and feel the sting of tears that want to come.

Quit stalling. Get in there.

I go up the walkway and open the door to a foyer painted a butter-yellow color, the bead-and-leaf molding a creamy white. There is a graceful chandelier hanging over a large round table, a bouquet of flowers at the center. I see parrot tulips and what look like Madame Hardy roses, but before I can examine what else is there, I hear my name being called.

I turn to see a forty-something woman who looks so calm, so full of peace. She has a warm, wide smile, and eyes that go way, way back. Soft brown hair, pulled back at the sides. A purple top and a blue cardigan over black slacks. A long silver necklace. When she shakes my hand, she puts her other hand on top of ours clasped together. However irrationally, I feel as though I understand a lot about the deliberateness of the way she lives.

"Cecilia Ross?"

"Yes," I say. "I go by Cece."

"I'm Annie Sullivan," she says, then adds, smiling, "Yup, the same name as Helen Keller's Annie. Come on in."

Her office is furnished with a desk and chair, and a soft, salmon-colored sofa and two chairs grouped around a coffee table on which are piles of literature, the kind featuring smiling people on the front whom you suspect are smiling *in spite of.*

"So tell me, Cece. What brings you here?"

"Well," I say, "I'm looking for a volunteer position."

"Uh-huh."

"And . . . this seems like it would be a good place to volunteer."

She nods. Waits.

"Because . . . Well, I've heard you do really good work." For some reason, although I'd intended to, I don't want to mention Penny. Maybe I fear I will get too emotional. Or maybe I want this to be a cleaner venture than that: me doing something I want to, rather than something I've been directed or persuaded to do.

"I think we do do good work, thank you for saying so. First, why don't I tell you a little about who our clients are and what our volunteers do, and then you can let me know if it seems like the right place for you."

"That's fine."

I listen to her talk about the clients, people who have chosen not to continue treatments for a terminal situation, who have opted instead for palliative care, comfort measures. She tells me that sometimes patients are here for a few months or even longer, sometimes for only a couple of days. Then she tells me about the volunteers: people who come to read to clients, or to bathe them, or to watch movies with them. To take them for walks, if they're able, or for brief car rides.

"We also have people who don't have direct contact," Annie says. "They do things like bake cookies for our clients and their family members. And for the staff, I'm happy to say!"

"Sounds . . ." I start to say, then realize I have no idea what to say next. "Nice!" I manage, and feel myself flushing at the inanity.

Will you calm down? Just listen.

"We also have volunteers who just sit with our clients. They literally just sit and don't do much of anything. Oftentimes they don't say anything, either."

"That I could do," I say, overly brightly, and we both laugh.

"Seriously," I say. "I could do that. Is it for people who are unconscious?"

"Not always. Sometimes we'll get a client who just doesn't really want to talk, but who derives a kind of comfort from someone just being there."

That would be easy enough, I think. But then, as though she's read my mind, Annie says, "It's not always easy."

"I would like to try it, though."

"When are you available to start?"

"I'm planning a short trip for the near future, but after that, I could volunteer at least twice a week, maybe more often. Also . . . Well, it may be helpful for you to know that I'm a motivational speaker."

"I think you'll find that it's a very unique kind of learning that goes on here. It never stops, really. In any case, no matter who they are, we do have a requirement that all our volunteers go through a background check as well as two six-hour training classes, held on the last weekend of every month. Is that all right with you?"

"Yes, that's fine."

Two days away—I can do it before I leave. I want to do it—the longer I sit here the more I feel I really want to work here.

Annie is frowning at something she's pulled up on the computer. "Hmm. Well, this month's class is full, but I could put you down for next month. I can send you home with an application."

"I'll fill it out right now, if that's okay."

"Of course." She gives me the application, which I fill out while she does paperwork of her own. Then she takes me on a brief tour to show me the ten rooms they have here. Several of the doors are open, and I can see into the rooms, see the various ways they've been decorated, or not. All of the beds are covered with colorful bedspreads or quilts. Most rooms have pictures of loved ones, plants or flowers, and some people have knickknacks or artwork here and there. There is a huge stuffed dog at the foot of one bed where a man lies snoring. Just looking at him, you'd never suspect anything is wrong. I remember a time I was riding in Penny's car with her when she was first diagnosed and someone cut her off. She looked over at me and smiled ruefully. Later, when she got weaker and looked bad, people gave sympathetic glances and a wide berth. "I liked it better when nobody knew," she said.

I see butterflies hanging from strings attached to the ceiling in one room where a woman smiles at me from her bed. My heart lurches at how extremely pale she is, at the frankness of her bald head. In the corner of her room, a plug-in fountain gently burbles, and I hear the sound of birds singing, as though they are right in there with her. I look over at Annie, and she says, "CD. It's lovely, isn't it?"

When clients smile at me, I find it surprising and humbling, too, in a very specific sort of way. Strange to think of it like this, perhaps, but it's as though the novitiate comes suddenly upon the master. Other clients, though, look like they are long past smiling. There's one, a man of about thirty years old who's heartbreakingly thin and has dark circles under his eyes so dramatic they look drawn in. He looks out at us as we walk past, and Annie says softly, "Hi, Michael." He says nothing back; his expression is empty of any emotion. "Excuse me for a moment," she tells me, and she goes up to Michael's bedside and speaks quietly to him. He does not respond. She touches his shoulder, then his arm, and leaves his room, comes back to me. "Let me show you the kitchen," she says. "And then I'll take you out to the garden."

Annie takes me next to a kitchen that can be used by both staff and clients. There's a small table in there, with a lamp on it, and Annie tells me they leave it on all night.

There's a chapel, stained-glass windows in shades of blue and red and yellow, a bench with kneelers. She shows me where the bathrooms are located on the main floor, introduces me to Florence, a smiling Hispanic woman who looks to be about my age, at the reception desk.

"So," Annie says. "There's your tour. Do you have any questions?"

I don't ask about Michael. Not yet. But I want to.

"We'll see you at the orientation, then," Annie says, and I thank her, shake her hand. Her grip is firm.

There is a jarring kind of brightness you experience coming out of a theater in the afternoon that I experience coming out of the Arms now. It has nothing to do with light, though.

I get back in the car and the radio now feels like so much noise. I turn it off. This feeling I'm having now has to do with that, how I want back inside something I've just experienced: a silence that contains everything you want to hear.

WHEN I GET HOME, I find a note from Renie on the kitchen table:

There's a letter for you. We'll be expecting a full report. Thanks for last night. So to speak.

I rush to the front table and grab the letter. It's a fat one! I bring it out to the front porch, sit down in one of the chairs, and open it.

It's not a long letter, only one page. But there are photographs:

that's what accounts for the thickness. I suspect the photographs will speak more to me, and I suspect, too, that that's what he intended.

I unfold the page, aware of a rush of joy that here his handwriting is again, in the here and now.

Cecilia,

So good to hear from you. I remember receiving letters from you before I went to Tahiti and I took that raft down the Amazon, and here would come a motorboat, sent to overtake me, and some guy would hand me a letter, and it got to be so that the three others on the raft with me would want to hear your letters, too, so I'd read them aloud. Then we'd all get quiet. Your heart's always on your sleeve, Cecilia, I always liked that about you.

First of all, I'm not married. First and last, I suppose, so don't think there's any need for censoring. Say whatever you like.

It's certainly a different life here than in Tahiti. I came back because my mom died, but also for reasons apart from that. But it'll take some getting used to, being back in this country: strange politics here, strange attitudes. I'm a little tired of talking about Tahiti, all those people who want to know what it was like, living there, what was it like? Everything I want to say is in my photos. Or in my actions, I suppose, the point is I'm not much of a word man. But then you know that, I'm sure.

I remember a lot, too, Cece.

As for coming to see me, I don't know, why not, come ahead. I'll shine my shoes, we'll go out dancing.

Dennis

Given the circumstances, it's a little frustrating not to be able to call him, but there is something about the pace of letter writing that's a welcome antidote to the speed of modern life. By their very nature, letters allow for more consideration of the words and thoughts that someone is offering you, in part because they prevent interruption. Perhaps best of all is their *keeping* quality—there were nights after Dennis left when I slept with pages he'd sent me from South America, and I felt as though I were with him, at least to the extent that I could be.

So I'll write back telling him I'll leave in a week. That will give me time to get ready, and also give some time to anyone else who might want to come with me. Then I'm off.

I read his letter again. Laugh out loud. And then I turn to the photographs.

They must be of where he is living now; they are at any rate certainly not taken in Tahiti. I see a young girl doing a cartwheel on her front lawn, her ponytails hanging upside down, her friend standing beside her, arms akimbo. On the front porch steps is an older woman, the child's grandmother, perhaps, her chin in her hands, and here is where my eye is drawn: I think I see in the grandmother's face a joyful recollection of doing cartwheels herself.

I asked Dennis once why he made photographs. I assumed it was because of the stories pictures tell, and the idea of something ephemeral being preserved. And that certainly was part of it. But what attracted him most was that cameras could record light. He said he was and would forever be a student of light, that the two things one uses, that one must have, in order to make a photograph are light and time.

He also told me that when he was in fifth grade, his teacher gave a slide show of modern art. Dennis was a poor student, probably dyslexic, though not diagnosed as such; it was not so easily recognized then. But at that moment, sitting at his desk in a darkened classroom that smelled of chalk and paper and baloney from the sandwich stored in his lunch box, he, in his words, took a trip to the Other. He realized he could explain everything he felt in a single image. Everything he felt and *was*.

There are a good twenty photographs, all scenes I imagine are from in or around his neighborhood. There's an old woman wearing a stained coat and backless slippers and carrying what must be a heavy shopping bag—she's listing to the left. She's shot from behind, and you can see an old-fashioned roller she must have forgotten, hanging from a piece of hair. Another photo is birds on a wire like notes on a staff, all facing forward but for the one on the end, who looks in that respect like a period at the end of a sentence. There are cirrus clouds so thin they look like bits of tissue paper glued to the sky and a shot of water braiding itself as it travels down a gutter. I'm going through the stack for the second time when my cellphone rings.

It's Annie Sullivan at the Arms, asking if I've a moment to talk.

"Of course," I say.

"I know I told you that we had no openings in the training class until next month."

"Yes."

"What I'm calling about is another matter, rather urgent. It has to do with a young man named Michael, whom you may recall from your visit here. He's the one I went in and spoke to."

"I do remember him." *You spoke to him and he acted as if you weren't even there.*

"Well, Michael has never asked for anything, but he did just now ask me for a favor and I wondered if you'd be interested in helping us accommodate him. He's been clear from the start that he wanted no visitors. That hasn't changed. But he's suddenly gotten very anxious about his wish being violated. What he wants is someone to simply sit in his room from eleven to one and from five to seven every day.

There's someone who's quite insistent on trying to see him, and she often tries to come on her lunch hour or after work. I've talked to her a few times, but she seems unwilling to give up. She's actually Michael's fiancée, or was, and she's a very nice woman, but a bit stubborn, as it turns out. As much as I would like to let her see him, I have to honor his wishes. I have volunteers who can sit with him in the evening, but not during the day. Could you? We could do a mini-training, just to give you some basics. But you'd mostly be just sitting there in what we call open attendance—he's never much talked to anyone. What do you think, does this seem like something you could do?"

"Well, I'll be leaving in a week."

"A week will be enough," she says, and I wonder if she doesn't expect Michael to live longer than that, or if it will just buy her enough time to find someone else. I agree to come tomorrow at ten, so that I can have the little training I'll get, and then I'll sit with him.

"Do you knit?" Annie asks.

"No. Why?"

"You'll probably need something to do."

"I'll bring something to read."

I hang up, then go to stand by the window and look outside. Such a young man.

One day when I was sad about something, Dennis came over, saw my face, and said, "Come with me."

"Where?" I asked, and he said, "To where I'm taking you."

Where he took me was down by the Mississippi River, to a wrought-iron entryway with an arched gate, LUCY WILDER MORRIS PARK inscribed in an elegant script at the top. No fence, just a gate, seemingly sticking out of nowhere. "This is a park?" I asked.

He told me that in the spring, there were wildflowers everywhere in this three-tenths-of-an-acre park, and he began naming them for me: Columbine. Wood anemone. White baneberry. Bittersweet night-shade. I remember when he said "Pipsissewa," I laughed. And he said it was an Abnaki word that meant "flower of the woods." That its colors were a near Day-Glo pink and purple.

I asked Dennis if later he would write the names of the flowers down for me. I knew I could find them in a field guide, but I wanted those flowers' names written out in his hand, so that I could hear him say them again every time I looked at his list. Also I wanted to go to his house when we were finished there, I wanted to get into bed with him and put my arms around him and the smartweed and the night-shade and the wild roses and the pyrola.

In my senior year, he took that rafting trip down the Amazon. The night before he left, he came to see me, late, and asked me to cut a lock of my hair and give it to him, which I readily did, of course I did: the lateness of the hour, the fullness of the moon, the nearness of his departure, the candle burning in the Chianti bottle, our knees press-ing hard together as we sat at the tiny kitchen table. He wound the long piece of my black hair into a knotted oval, then put it in a raw-hide pouch that he wore around his neck. And I remember that I asked no questions that night, nothing about what else was in that pouch, or had been in there, or why he wore it, or why he wanted a lock of my hair in it. I cut off a piece my hair, I gave it to him, he nod-ded, and I nodded back.

After he left, days would come when I missed him so, and I'd go down to Lucy Wilder Morris Park to find him again. I'd bring along the piece of paper torn from one of his sketchbooks, on which he'd written the names of the wildflowers. Bloodroot, whose flowers lasted only a day or two. Field bindweed, which looked like tiny morning glories. Milkweed, in which the monarchs laid their eggs. He wrote down *blue vervain, lady's slippers, butter-and-eggs, four-o'clocks.* When he wrote down *harebells,* he told me that they looked delicate, but that they could grow between rocks. He wrote down *forget-me-nots,* and I said, "I'll never forget you." And he turned his head and looked at me, and with that look said, *Nor I you.*

I snap Riley's leash on. "Hey," I say. "Want to go for a walk?"

I'll take him to Como Park, through the woods by the golf course where we'll be able to catch a glimpse of the conservatory. Lucy Wilder Morris Park isn't there anymore. The area has been cleaned up and modernized, which for me means that the charm and the wonder are gone. The wrought-iron gate, that fairy-tale entrance not only to a park but to a way of thinking, is long gone. Some things we really ought to keep.

THAT NIGHT MY ROOMMATES AND I ARE OUT ON THE PORCH HAVING a picnic dinner that I made: wrap sandwiches with hummus and raw vegetables, corn on the cob, sliced tomatoes, potato salad, and watermelon drizzled with aged balsamic. Afterward, Joni goes to have a drink with a man she recently met at the restaurant, telling us not to wait up for her, and Renie goes to a movie that I've already seen and that Lise doesn't want to see. We linger together on the porch, I in the hammock, Lise stretched out on the swing. The days are lengthening, there's the scent of cut grass in the air.

"It's so nice out tonight," I tell Lise, and she agrees, but in a distracted way.

"You okay?" I ask. I know she's been worried about a young patient of hers who's having kidney problems.

"If it's still all right with you," she says, "I do want to go on the road trip with you and Renie. I've got nine weeks of vacation to use up, so that's no problem. But now I'm not sure I should visit the person I was thinking of seeing."

"Who is it?"

"My ex." She shrugs. "I've been thinking a lot about him, about us. He wasn't the nicest guy in the world. But I wasn't, either, is the thing. I don't think I ever stepped up to recognizing my part in our coming undone. And I think I made a lot of mistakes with our daughter, with Sandy, having to do with him. I thought I was so very careful not to badmouth him, and I never did, not directly. But I made it clear that I didn't think much of him, when he's . . . he's her *father*. And the truth is, there's a lot to like about him. We just didn't . . . I don't know. We got married so young. And I used to blame him every time I was upset about anything. I was so critical! I think I just wore him down. I complained because he wouldn't open up to me but then every time he did, I just . . . Well, I was very critical.

"When we split, when we were in court the day we were granted the divorce, it felt to me like we were in a play of some kind. It just was so unreal. And after it was over, when we came outside, he said something I barely heard, it was as though I were underwater. But what he said was an apology. He was apologizing for the way we'd failed each other, the way we'd hurt each other, the way we hadn't been able to rescue ourselves from such terrible ruin. And you know what I said? I shook his hand and said, 'We'll be in touch about Sandy.' "

She sighs. "There's so much I didn't realize about what divorce does. For one thing, it doesn't go away. It doesn't go *away*.

"Sandy sees him at least once a month and I don't know what they talk about, but for so long now she's been incredibly hostile to me. It might not have anything to do with Steven, it might just be her age—when I was twenty, I hated my mother as a matter of principle; her *breathing* pissed me off. Or it might be Sandy's own problems that I'm not aware of—she doesn't talk to me like she used to.

"Whatever it is, things are just so cold between us, and oftentimes I wish I could talk to someone who really knows her. Someone who knew her when she was that sweet little girl in her favorite patent leather shoes, holding on to her blankie. The preteen who used my baster as a microphone to sing Madonna songs in front of her mirror. And the only person who shares all those memories of her is my ex."

Lise has been staring into the night, talking, but now she turns to look at me. "What do you think about my going to see him?"

"I think it's up to you and him."

"Yeah. I wonder what he'd be like with me."

"It's hard to say, I guess."

"I also wonder if I have other motives, ones I haven't admitted to myself."

We fall silent, and then she says, "Cece? Would you go and get your box?"

When Renie comes home, we tell her: Lise is coming on the road trip. Just to go, but also maybe to see someone.

"And then they were three," Renie says.

"DO YOU REMEMBER MARY LOU SINGLETON?" MY MOTHER ASKS me. I've come to visit her before I go to the Arms. And I did call ahead.

"The woman with the little black dog?"

"Right. Fala. Well, she died. Mary Lou, not Fala."

"Oh, I'm sorry. You liked her, right?"

"She was nice. I used to play Chicken Feet with her." A card game a lot of the residents here enjoy.

"Was it . . . sudden?" I ask.

My mother shrugs. "No death is sudden, here. If you know what I mean."

"I guess not."

Then, to change the subject, I say, "Hey. Do you remember Dennis Halsinger?"

She sniffs and looks away from me. We're sitting in the vast dining room, and we're the only ones here. There's coffee available all the time, and it's delicious; I like to sit here with my mom sometimes and have some. There's a nice view of the garden outside the glass doors, and birds come regularly to the feeder they have out there. Squirrels, too, and one of the women goes after them with a broom.

"Dennis Halsinger was that hippie. You always seemed to think so much of him."

"Yes, I did."

"He was a handsome young man, but he didn't take care of himself."

"He took care of himself!"

"Oh, he wore those leather vests with no shirt and his hair was much too long. And he wore necklaces."

"He wore *a* necklace. Which many men do now. Including your beloved Twins."

"Well, his was a hippie necklace. But why are you asking about him? Have you heard from him?"

"Yes, I have, I got a letter out of the blue, and I'm going to go and see him."

"Doesn't he live in Hawaii?"

"He was in Tahiti, but he's in Cleveland now."

"Cleveland! What's he doing there?"

"He came back because . . ." I don't want to say his mother died. "He missed being in the States."

"Well, you do what you want. The one I always liked was Greg Larson."

"I know you did."

"Cece?"

Here it comes, I think. She'll ask me why I don't try to find Greg Larson. But I am wrong. What she says is "Would you have any feelings about my getting married again?"

Spencer Thompson? Big ears? "Would I have any *feelings* about it?" I say.

"Shhh!" my mother says, looking around.

"There's no one here," I say.

"People wander in."

I lower my voice, lean in closer to her. "Of course I would have feelings about it! Is that what you want to do, get married again?"

"It's not for love and romance so much as it is for practical reasons. You should hear your father carry on every time I use that step stool to reach up to the top shelves in the kitchen."

"Why are you reaching up into those shelves? We specifically organized your kitchen so that you wouldn't have to go up there. All that's up there is holiday dishes, and you know I'll come and get them out when you need them."

"And he's worried about my being alone so much."

"You're not alone so much!"

"Well, that's exactly what I told him. But he feels I'd be better off with someone around. Especially at night."

"Ma, if you want to get married, I'm glad for you. It's just taking me a little by surprise."

"Well, me, too."

"You mean, when he asked you?"

"No. I mean when your father told me to get married. I haven't been asked yet. I've got to think about who I might want."

Meet my mother.

"Tell me honestly, honey, what do you think is more important, money or sex appeal? Mary Lou always said a sense of humor, but you know that won't pay the bills."

"Good luck, Ma," I say, and she says, "You, too."

I'm not sure, but I think I liked it better when she was my mother and not my girlfriend.

Annie Sullivan and I have gone over a few things for our brief training session, which mostly is focused on communication. She has coached me in listening techniques—reflection, clarification, and so on—and impressed on me the importance of a silence that is active, that suggests a kind of willingness and acceptance. "And when you speak, err on the side of brevity," she said.

She told me about what posture conveys on the parts of both the client and the attendant, how it is important that you not seem put upon. She told me that grief takes many forms, from hilarity to hostility, and to be willing to accept what may seem like odd behavior as being completely normal, under the circumstances. She said that sometimes when a person's body is ready to stop, even wanting to stop, the person will nonetheless linger because of important or unresolved issues.

Most of this I already knew and was comfortable with. But then she told me what to do if Michael seemed to be in pain, if he vomited, if he lost control of his bladder or bowels. He probably would not ask for anything, including food or drink; he had been eating very little, but just so I knew, he was allowed anything he wanted in the way of food. I nodded, but for the first time I felt nervous. I wondered if I should be doing this after all. There was a reason that my first reaction when Penny suggested it was one of incredulity.

"One last thing," Annie says now. "Perhaps the most important thing. You need to be honest. These clients are very sensitive to artifice of any kind, they don't have time for that. Okay?"

"Yes."

She pushes back in her chair, puts her hands flat on her desk, and says, "So. There's our crash course. Any questions?"

"No. Not yet, anyway."

"Call on any of the staff if you need us for anything."

"I will."

We stand, shake hands, and she says, "Thanks for stepping in this way. It will give me a few days to train someone else to take over when you leave."

I nod, start to leave the office, and she calls my name.

"One last thing. You should know that he probably won't or can't thank you. Don't take it personally."

"Oh, I don't expect him to thank me," I say. "I only want to help if I can."

I follow her upstairs, and she is leading me to Michael's room when her pager goes off. "He's right there," she says, pointing to the room a few steps away. I recall it from my last visit. "I've got to go. Are you okay?"

I nod.

I go to his room and knock lightly on the open door. He is turned away, but when he hears the knock, he turns toward me.

"I'm Cecilia Ross," I say. "Cece."

He stares at me.

"I'm here to—"

"I know why you're here. Have a seat."

I go to the chair by the window and put my purse on the windowsill. When I turn around, his eyes are closed. I sit down and wait.

Two hours later, I haven't done anything but stand guard, wait to see if Michael will open his eyes or speak, and read to myself from the book I brought along. As I stand to leave, I hear him say something. "Pardon?" I say. I walk to the side of the bed, lean in closer. "I'm sorry; I didn't hear you."

"I said thank you." Two words that, coming from him, assume an entirely disproportionate weight.

"You're welcome," I say. I had wanted to do so much more for him.

As I am almost out the door, I hear him say, "You'd never think it would be boring, right?"

I turn around. "I wasn't bored!"

"I am."

"Oh! Oh, well, I . . ."

What to say? I think of Annie telling me that it's important to be honest, and so I am honest. I say, "I hadn't thought of that. Would you like me to maybe read to you next time?"

"When's next time?"

"Tomorrow."

He sighs. "Yes."

"Anything in particular?"

"Oh," he says, "I don't know." He points to the book I have under my arm. "Is that poetry?"

I nod.

"Maybe that."

"Do you have any favorite poets?"

An immense sorrow comes into his face.

"How about if I just bring a variety?" I ask quickly. "Jane Hirshfield, Billy Collins, Marie Howe?"

"Charles Simic?"

"Of course. I'll bring him, too."

He nods. "Good."

"Tomorrow, then." I hold my hand up, and he does the same, then closes his eyes again.

At the end of the hall, I see a young woman with long blond hair in a ponytail. She's wearing a stylish trench coat, a blue silk dress beneath it, low heels. She carries a briefcase and a purse. Michael's fiancée! I stop short, thinking, *I'll go back to his room. If she tries to come in, I'll gently rebuff her. If that doesn't work, I'll call out for staff.* But then she opens the door to another room and I hear her say, "Grandma?"

Embarrassed by my apparent willingness to gin up for war, I continue on my way.

In the lobby, I see Annie, and she smiles and comes over. "So?"

"It was fine," I say.

"No sign of his fiancée?"

"No, although I saw a young woman I thought at first might be her. But she went into another room."

Annie frowns. "I'm sorry; I completely forgot to tell you what Phoebe looks like."

"That's her name? Phoebe? What a lovely, old-fashioned name."

"Yes, and she seems to be a lovely, old-fashioned girl. Very sweet and gentle, except when it comes to her determination to see someone who clearly does not want to see her."

I nod, then say, "But . . . is it so clear, really?"

"It is, unfortunately. In his three weeks here, he has never vacillated. I suppose he has his own reasons. He won't talk about her other than to say he doesn't want to see her. At all. And she's the only one who has come to visit."

"His family? Does he not have family?"

"His parents are dead, and he didn't care to name anyone else as a relative. And if he has friends, he must have asked that they not come, either. It may be hard to understand, but I have to take him at his word when he says that that's the way he wants it. Did he talk to you at all?"

"He did. Just as I was leaving. It's funny . . . he said he was bored."

Annie nods. "I've heard that before. One woman told me that even the pain got boring. I asked if it helped to have visitors, and she said, 'It's not that kind of boredom.' "

Now it's my turn to nod. I'm not sure exactly what that woman meant, yet I feel the truth of her words. I tell Annie, "We agreed that I would read some poetry to him tomorrow."

"Wonderful."

"So . . . what *does* Phoebe look like?"

"Oh, she's lovely. Long blond hair. Tall and quite slender. Always well dressed."

I swallow. "That was her, then! I think it was! But she went into a room two doors down, the one at the end of the hall."

"That room is empty."

Quickly, we go together up the stairs and down the hall to the room Phoebe went into. No one is there. Then we go on to Michael's room, where he lies sleeping. Annie tiptoes in and checks the bathroom. She shakes her head no when she comes out. We go back downstairs and she walks me to the door.

"Well, you'll know for tomorrow," Annie says.

"I'm sorry," I say.

"Not your fault! She came late today, though. I'll have to remember that." She sighs. "She had given up for a while; she didn't come five days in a row, as far as I know. But here she is, back at it. If I can catch her, I'll try talking to her. Again."

THAT NIGHT, I'M IN MY ROOM, THINKING ABOUT SEEING DENNIS, wondering what we'll say to each other. What does anyone say to anybody who used to be so important in her life, whom she's not seen in such a long time? It seems to me that in situations like this, we're all wondering the same thing: *I'm still me; are you still you?*

A woman named Nancy who drove me around Cincinnati at one of my speaking gigs had just gotten back from a business trip to Miami. She said she'd heard an old boyfriend lived there, and she found him online, then called him to see if he'd like to get together for old times' sake. She was divorced and sick of the men she was meeting on Match.com, and she really wanted to spend a little time with an attractive guy she felt safe with. She called his home and he answered the phone and she said, very tentatively, "Hi, is this Ben?" and he yelled, *"Nance?"*—he remembered her, just like that.

They both started laughing and then talking a mile a minute; she said it was like no time at all had passed, they might as well have been back in high school, where he used to walk her to class and be late for his own so often they finally stopped giving him detention slips. After they talked awhile, she told him she was coming to Miami and asked if they could meet for coffee. He said he'd have to ask his wife, which sort of doused the flames, but she held on while he did ask, thinking she'd wear blue, he'd always liked her in blue.

The wife said no. Even after Nancy got on the phone with her to say that she was just an old friend and the wife was welcome to come, too. No, the wife said, she didn't think it was a good idea.

When Ben got back on the phone to say goodbye, Nancy gave him the address of her hotel, but he never showed, never called.

"I mean, I suggested *coffee,* not even a *drink,*" she said. "Meeting for *coffee,* what's wrong with that?"

I raised an eyebrow, and she sighed and said, "I know."

A knock on the door, and I say, "Come in."

It's Joni. She comes over and sits at the foot of my bed. "I have to get a bunch of new clothes."

"Oh? Why?"

"I'm in love. I might be in love. I really like this guy. Jeffrey Mitchell. Isn't that a nice name?"

"Yes, it is. Good for you!"

"Yeah. I want to get some new clothes and all new makeup. Even new socks, I saw the cutest socks, and you know what was on them? Whisks! I'm going to get them and a whole bunch of other things, some really pretty dresses, too."

"And you're going to lose ten pounds, right?"

She looks at me. "You think I need to lose ten pounds?"

"No, it's just something that so many women say when they meet a guy they like."

"Well, I don't have to lose weight."

"I know."

"Maybe five pounds."

"Not even that."

She leans toward me, embracing herself. "I'm excited."

"I know."

"I mean, *really excited!*" she squeals.

"Yes, I can see that."

"Well. Good night."

"Good night."

When she gets to the door, she turns around. "I'm kind of embarrassed, being this excited—and at this age!"

"You're in good company." I slide down to rest my head on my pillow. I wonder how much weight I can lose in a week. Once, I put the pedal to the metal and lost seven pounds in a week, but then I got scared that I had some deadly disease and ate a pizza just to make sure and three pounds came right back on. And then, of course, the other four.

IN THE MORNING, I DRESS AND SHOWER EARLY, THEN COME DOWN-stairs just as Renie is leaving.

"I'm going in for a meeting at the paper," she says. She puts on her raincoat and belts it tightly. "Guess what. I got an email from her this morning."

"Your daughter?"

"Yes."

"What'd she say?"

"She'd rather not see me. As I elected quite a while ago not to have anything to do with her. Also, she thinks the name Camille is just weird and why did I even tell her that. Also, she is not about to dishonor her real mother by seeing me."

"It wouldn't be dishonoring her mother!"

"Yeah." She stands still, considering. "She hates me. I don't blame her. It's what I expected. It's what I deserve." She shrugs, picks up her briefcase, and walks out before I can say what I think is true: her daughter will change her mind.

"We'll talk about it tonight," I call after her, but I'm not sure she's heard me.

"Talk about what?" Lise asks, coming into the kitchen and pouring herself a cup of coffee.

"Renie and her daughter," I say.

Lise turns to look at me. "What happened?"

"I think we should all talk about it at once, if Renie wants to."

She sits at the table, studies me. "Were you a Brownie?"

"Yes."

"A Girl Scout?"

I hesitate, then say, "Yes."

"Did you also get good grades in comportment?"

"Comportment!"

"Yeah, didn't they used to have comportment on report cards?"

I say nothing. They did used to have something like that, but I can't remember *what* they called it.

"Go to work," I say.

"You need to learn to gossip better," Lise says.

"I know how to gossip; don't you worry about me."

"Renie's not the only one having problems," Lise says. "I told Sandy last night that I was going to see her father and did not exactly get the response I was hoping for. She had, as they say, a fit."

"Why?"

She sighs. "She wants to protect him, I suppose."

"From what?"

"From me. From my awfulness. I am an awful person, just ask her."

I sit there for a moment, then say, "Okay, you want to gossip?"

"Not about my daughter."

"I don't like how she treats you. Can I say that?"

"No. She wasn't always like this. Once she told me I was her golden mommy. Only she said *goden*. She also said—and I thought this was profound—'When you're done being my mommy, I'll be your mommy.' She had such sweet curls at the back of her neck and she smelled like sugar cookies. I loved her so much. The first time she got a cold I slept by her crib. I got up every hour to listen to her lungs to make sure she wasn't getting pneumonia."

"You know, Lise, you don't need her permission to go and see your ex or to do anything else."

"Oh, I'm going to see him. I emailed him and he was . . . Well, he didn't say no."

"Good."

"I'm going!"

"Good!"

"I just wanted her to be happy about it. I want her to be happy, period. I just want all the time for her to be happy."

"I know." It occurs to me to say that if Lise would stop lobbying so hard for her daughter's happiness, Sandy might find it on her own. And if she finds her own happiness, she might stop taking her discontent out on her mother. But what do I know. I can hardly manage Riley, whose wet muzzle is on my chin, his eyes rolled up in entreaty. "I got nothing," I tell him.

He wags his tail.

I hold up my empty hands.

He walks away, drops into a heap in a corner of the kitchen, rests his muzzle on his crossed paws, and sighs through his nose. After Lise leaves the room, I get a piece of bread and give him one half of it, then the other. "Don't tell," I say. Riley weighs too much. No one else in this house is old enough to understand that there comes a time when you are at peace with such things. Penny used to say she slept with her belly like a lover, her arms wrapped around it. "You old fatty," I say to Riley, and he thumps his tail.

I take my empty dishes to the sink to rinse them off. *Conduct!* That's what it was called.

"YOU DON'T MISS YOUR HOUSE?" MICHAEL ASKS. I'VE FILLED him in on a little of my background, including the fact that I recently moved in with three other women.

"I miss it a little, every now and then," I say. "But I realize I was ready to move long before I did."

I smile at him. I brought him some Tootsie Pops and he has one stuck in his cheek; he looks like a lopsided chipmunk.

"It's just the stage I've come to," I say. "I never thought I wouldn't want all these things I worked hard to get. But . . ." I shrug. "They weren't it. It turns out to be true that what matters—"

"I get it," he says and looks away from me. He takes the pop from his mouth and lays it on the nightstand.

A moment, and then he says, "Anyway. Going from living alone for so long to living with so many others—wasn't that weird for you?"

"It just seems natural, and it did from the very beginning. I guess I miss not having to compromise about anything. But it's offset by so many good things. I find I like the company. I've come to rely on it, in fact.

"But mostly . . . Well, life is always changing, right? And I think it's human nature to be fearful of change. Even if the changes you dread most end up being the ones that are best. That's what happened to me, anyway."

"Yeah. For me, I guess I'm a little worried that I . . . that I . . . Wait a second. Hold on." He puts his hand up to his forehead, touches it lightly, touches it again, then puts his hand back at his side.

"Michael, are you . . . Do you need something for pain?"

"Not yet."

"I could go and ask for something for you. Annie told me it's important to not let the pain get too bad before taking something."

"Oh. Is that what Annie said?" His tone has become sharp.

"You just seemed to get really uncomfortable."

"The pain medication makes me go to sleep," Michael says. "And I don't want to go to sleep now."

"I understand. But you'll let me know if—"

"I'll take care of getting something when I want it. What with it being *my decision.*"

A moment. And then I say, "Okay. Good. Then I can goof off a little more. I mean, this is too much work, running around and getting you this, getting you that. I'm exhausted."

He smiles. "So, what, are you retired?"

"I'm taking some time off."

"What do you do?"

"I'm a motivational speaker."

"Ah. I guess that fits."

"It does, huh?"

"Anybody besides your parents ever die on you?" he asks, abruptly.

The question is so sudden and out of the blue, I answer it before thinking: "Yes. My best friend. Fairly recently—a few months ago. Penny was her name."

"I'm sorry."

"Thank you."

"Were you with her in the time leading up to it?"

"Yes."

"Was it hard? Didn't it just make you sadder, seeing her decline that way?"

"Well, of course it was sad. But also . . .

"Look, I know how this might sound, Michael. But also it was one of the most beautiful experiences of my life, and I am so grateful for having been with her. For me to have been there just *in case*, you know? And to try to tell her in every way how much she meant to me. Before, then, always."

"Do you ever . . ." He looks at me, his face full of longing, of such delicate weariness. "Do you ever see her? You know what I mean? Do you ever see her?"

"I feel her. And I believe I hear her."

"Really?"

"Really. Not often, but . . . sometimes. I don't tell everyone that, but it's true." I pause, then say, "I suppose it might be my own voice I'm hearing, some thought that comes from me that I assign to her. Who knows? I guess I don't want to know. Or need to."

Michael winces, touches his head again, then presses the call bell. His hand is trembling now.

I stand. "I'm sorry, I should have—"

"Just keep talking," he says.

Just then, a nurse in a pale pink smock appears. She goes over to Michael and turns off the call light. "Need some pain medication?" she asks, gently.

"Yeah, I do."

"I'll be right back."

Michael looks over at me. "So tell me about your friend."

I smile. "Well, she was smart and perceptive and she had no prob-

lem letting you know what she thought about things. She was *fun*.
She would take chances. Once, on a hot summer day we—"

"*Fuck!*"

"Michael."

"*What?*"

"I let you wait too long. I'm sorry."

He closes his eyes again. "Not your fault. It will get better. Oh,
Jesus, *fuck!* Sorry. Sorry. It will get better."

I have no idea what to do. Stay? Go? But then the nurse comes
back and says, "I'll take care of him. Thank you."

I gather my things. "I'll see you tomorrow, okay?"

"Yes," he says, from between clenched teeth, as the nurse turns
him on his side to give him an injection. "Cece?"

"Yes?"

"What did you . . . on the hot day, what did you . . . ?"

"Oh. We broke into someone's backyard and went swimming in
their pool."

"Cool."

"We were in there for forty minutes before one of the teenagers
who lived there came home. We told him we were from Pool Pros and
everything looked fine. And he thanked us and went inside, and
Penny and I went home and grilled hamburgers."

I see the nurse smile as she helps Michael onto his back and
straightens his covers. He closes his eyes and says, "See you tomorrow, Cece."

"See you tomorrow."

I stop by Annie's office in order to confess about letting Michael
wait so long for pain medication. But *did* I do something wrong?
She's not there. And anyway, he said yes, about seeing him tomorrow.

I walk home under a still gray sky, the air heavy with moisture. One thing about doing this kind of work, you develop a keen appreciation for the fact that you can walk. And see the sky. And feel the air on your face. And that you can check high and low and no, nothing in your body is hurting, not one thing.

I AWAKEN FROM A NAP to hear someone coming in the door, then hear an unfamiliar voice greeting Riley. I go downstairs and find a young woman standing there, dressed in jeans and a plain white T-shirt.

"Who're you?" she says.

I tell her, then wait for her to introduce herself. As I suspected, she's Lise's daughter, Sandy. She doesn't look like Lise at all: her features, her bone structure, are much coarser, though she is a very attractive young woman. She must take after her father.

"Is my mom here?"

"She's not home from work yet. She said she'd be late tonight; she's finishing up some things before we leave. We're going—"

"I know where you're going."

I nod, and she stands there.

"So . . . can I ask you something?" she says.

"Sure."

"Do you *like* my mom?"

I keep myself from reacting in any way. "Yes, I do. Very much."

Sandy shifts her weight, crosses her arms. "She's a good doctor."

"Yes, so I've gathered."

"Yup. She's interested in healing everyone but her own family."

I say nothing.

Sandy shrugs. "Never mind." She starts for the door.

"Should I have her call you?"

She doesn't turn around. "No."

"Tell her you stopped by?"

She looks over her shoulder at me. "Yeah. Tell her I stopped by to tell her not to go. Again."

"You know, maybe—"

"Or nothing. Tell her nothing. That's all she hears anyway."

I watch her go out to her red Corolla and drive away. I'll tell Lise her daughter stopped by to say goodbye, if I tell her anything.

I'M FINISHING UP a letter to Dennis when from downstairs I hear Renie call, "Hey, Cece!"

I open the door and stick my head out of my room. "Yes?"

"Can you help me make dinner?"

"Sure," I call back. "Two minutes."

I go back to the letter, where I've been telling Dennis about Michael. I finish the paragraph, then write:

I'll see you soon. Consider yourself mapquested.

When I come into the kitchen, Renie is at the stove, her back to me. "Okay. What do you need, you slacker?"

When she turns around, I regret having said it. Her face is full of misery. *I'll bet she got fired.* You can't be as out there as Renie and not expect that at some point it's going to catch up with you. "What happened?" I ask. "Did you get fired?"

Her face changes. "No! Why would I get fired?"

"I don't know."

"Why would they fire me? They *love* me!"

"Then . . . Your daughter?" I ask, and she turns back to the pot she's stirring.

"Chicken chili with salsa verde," she says. "Can you make the corn bread?"

"Is there a recipe?"

"On the cornmeal box. And yes, my daughter. I just had the brilliant idea of calling her."

"What did she say?"

"Not a lot. First hello, then . . . *Click!* Well, she didn't say 'click.' The phone did. On her behalf."

"Yeah, well, guess what?" I say.

"What?"

"I don't know, nothing." I had been going to say, *We're going to see her anyway.* But now that seems ill-advised. Especially when Renie says, "Forget my coming on the trip. I can help Joni watch Riley."

"He's coming. Lise is all excited about bringing him. He's getting ice cream at every Dairy Queen we pass."

"He'd probably rather have a hamburger. Before they cook it."

I get out the measuring cups. "How come Joni never measures anything?"

Renie snorts. "Once I asked her the same thing. She reached in the flour sack and said 'Okay, one third of a cup.' And she pulled out a handful and put it into the measuring cup. Exactly one third of a cup."

"So?" I say, and Renie says, "Yeah. Exactly. La-di-da. Who even cares. Are you done with the quarter-cup measure?"

We're about half an hour away from dinner when we hear the front door slam, then slam again. We stand still, waiting, and then Joni walks in. She's wearing her chef's jacket and her face is flushed.

She stands before us with her fists clenched. "Okay. There are two words I never want to hear again. *Chef* and *restaurant.*"

"What happened?" I say.

"Where's Lise?" she asks. "Get Lise down here. *Lise!*"

"She's not home yet," I say.

"What happened?" Renie asks.

"I'll tell you all at dinner. I'm only telling this once."

She starts to walk away, but then she comes back into the kitchen. "Okay. I just got yelled at for *nine minutes straight.* A sauce separated, and Gaetano yelled at me for *nine minutes straight.* In the kitchen, in front of everyone. Then he followed me into the walk-in and yelled at me some more. In the time that he yelled at me, I could have made three more sauces. I could have fixed the problem! But he wanted to yell at me because he loves to yell at me. And swear at me. And pound his fat fist into his fat hand half an inch from my face. So this time? I just walked right out of there. Right when I was supposed to baste the veal. I hope it's ruined. He told me I didn't have the skills to work at Denny's. He told me he was going to put me back on salad prep and that I should consider myself lucky for that. I am a very talented chef! *Person!* When I met Grant Achatz he asked if I wanted to come on at Alinea!" She starts to cry. "Now I won't have any health insurance. But I don't care. Because at least I will never have to be in that god-damn kitchen ever again. I am never taking that kind of abuse again. Never! I *quit!*"

She takes a breath. "Sorry to yell at you. I'm going up to take a shower. And I'm going on that road trip with you all. I am taking a vacation. Which I *so deserve.*"

She leaves the room, and Renie and I look at each other. And to think I thought it was Renie who was having problems at work.

I T'S THE NIGHT BEFORE OUR TRIP, AND WE'RE ALL SITTING AROUND the living room, too full to move. Joni made a spectacular pasta pesto and mission fig salad and every one of us overindulged.

"We should go to bed," Joni says. "We have to get up at five."

"I'm not getting up at five," Lise says. "Five-thirty."

"Five-fifty," I say.

Renie says nothing. She's been quiet all night. But then Joni asks again if she's sure she doesn't want to come, and it's as though a dam bursts. "What does she *think*?" she says. "Does she think I went into that hospital and delivered her and walked out and . . . and . . . went *shopping*? Which P.S. I hate under *any* circumstances? How can she believe I ever forgot about her? How can she think I didn't care? Why can't she see *my* side of it, how it was so hard for me to *do that,* how I did it for *her*?"

None of us answers.

"What kind of parents did she get, anyway? How could they raise such an insensitive child? And one with no apparent curiosity! Isn't she even curious? Why is she still living in Winona, is she ever going to leave Winona? I don't even . . . Is she even mine? Maybe I got the wrong information. My kid wouldn't be such a jerk. I'm her *mother,* doesn't she even want to see what I *look* like?"

Lise speaks up. "Maybe she—"

"I'm going to bed," Renie says. "Have a great time, you guys. I won't be getting up to send you off. But really, I hope you have a great time."

After she's left the room, Joni whispers, "Ten bucks she comes."

"You're on," Lise whispers back. To me, "You in?"

"No," I say.

It's not funny. Or at least it's nothing to bet on.

I go upstairs, too, wanting suddenly to be alone. I lie on my bed and look up at the ceiling, wondering if Renie will change her mind. I doubt it. I'm sorry about that. Without her, things won't be as much fun. If it were anyone else, I'd try to think of some way to persuade her. But Renie is the kind who has to come to things herself, or she won't come to them at all.

I'M UP EARLY, IN SPITE OF MYSELF. FOUR MINUTES OF FIVE. I turn on my bedside light, turn off the alarm, and sit at the edge of my bed, thinking about how we'll soon be on our way. In my nightstand drawer is Dennis's latest letter, received yesterday, and I read it again now.

> *Call me when you're about five minutes away. I'm going to station myself at the window, and if you're still good-looking, I'm not coming out. I've got some problems in the hair department, lost the main attraction there. The mane attraction. I've got some problems in the physique department, too. Think I won't elaborate too much there. Suffice it to say I know you've gotten older, but I've really gotten older.*

When I go into the kitchen after having taken a shower, I find Lise at the kitchen table. Something looks strange about her, and then I realize it's that she doesn't have her glasses on.

I get some coffee and slide into the booth with her, and she says, "What do you think?"

"About what?"

She points to her face.

"You mean no glasses?"

"Contacts."

"You got contacts?"

"Yesterday." She pushes her plate toward me. "Want half of an English muffin?"

I take a bite of muffin, look at her more carefully. "You look good. But you look good with glasses, too."

"I just thought, you know, when we were together, I didn't wear glasses."

She blows some air out of her cheeks. "You know, maybe I . . . I'm thinking of not going. It's probably a bad idea."

"No it isn't."

She looks sharply at me. "Do you really think you're the one to decide that?"

I shrug. "Guess not."

She gets up to refill her cup. "I'm sorry. It's just that . . ." She turns around, leans against the counter with her arms crossed. "I mean, as of now we're . . . cordial. And if I go to see him, I could do something that could screw things up and he could end up not talking to me at all."

"Or you could make things better. At least in terms of your daughter."

"Maybe."

"You don't have to see him. You could just come along for the ride. It'll be fun; we'll stop at every funky thing we find. Nobody ever had a bad time on a road trip; it's been well documented."

"Yeah," she says, but I can tell she's not really listening.

"How about if you don't decide about seeing him just yet? See how you feel when we get closer. You've taken time off from work for a vacation; take a vacation."

Riley hears the newspaper land on the front porch and runs to the door, barking. "Riley, *NO BARK!*" Lise yells, and runs to get him. "I don't want him to wake up Renie," she tells me, pulling him into the room with us.

"I don't know if he'll wake her up. *You* might."

"I wish she were coming," Lise says. "She was up late last night, I heard her banging around in her room and then she went downstairs for a while. I think she's really conflicted."

"Maybe we should make noise," I say. "What if she wakes up later and wishes she'd come with us?"

"I don't know."

"Joni, let's GO!" I yell.

"Shhhhhh!" we hear Joni say, and then her suitcase comes bumping down the steps before her. "Damn it!" she says, chasing after it.

"Well," I say, "she's certainly had her chance to wake up."

We go out into the pale colors of dawn to my SUV. We stash our bags in the way-back and take our places. I'll drive first, Lise will ride shotgun, Joni will be in the back with Riley. And with Renie, too, apparently, because just as I'm pulling away from the curb, we hear Renie calling, "Wait for me, wait for me, wait for me!" She's running after us in her hunting-dog pajamas and sneakers, her briefcase over her shoulder and banging into her hip. She jumps in the backseat and says, "What."

"You're coming in your pajamas?" Joni asks.

"I'll change later."

"Into what?"

Renie looks at her. "Into what I *buy* to *wear.*"

"You're going to buy everything you need?" I ask.

She straightens the collar of her pajama top, pushes her hair off her face. "Didn't you ever want to do that? Take a trip without packing one single thing?"

Silence. It seems that yes, we all have.

"First purchase, toothpaste," she says.

"You can borrow mine," Joni says, and Renie says, "Nope, I'm getting a kind I never had before. I'm doing that this whole trip."

"What kind of toothpaste have you never had before?" Lise asks.

"Licorice kind, there's a licorice kind."

"There is?" I ask.

"See?" Renie says. "Also, I'm getting a light-up toothbrush." Then, before we can ask, "Target, kids' section."

"So . . . Winona is two and half hours from here . . ." I say.

"Yes," Renie says. "I'm going to try. I just sent her an email that I would be at the Acoustic Café at noon."

"Where is it?" Lise asks.

"You're not coming. Nobody's coming. I'm going alone. I'll just go there and wait for one hour and see if she comes."

"We have to get you there," I remind her.

"I'll have you drop me around the corner," Renie says. "It's at 77 Lafayette."

"How will you recognize each other?" I ask.

"I said I'd put a rose on the table. It's stupid, but it's all I could think of. I'll find a rose somewhere."

"That's not stupid," I say.

We stop to gas up, and Lise puts the address in the GPS. Then we're all quiet, listening to NPR, until Renie says, "You know that saying *Be kind, for everyone is carrying a heavy burden*? It's not true."

"Yes, it is," I say.

"Not necessarily," Joni says.

"Depends on how you define *burden*," Lise says. And then, "Oh, look, cows. Riley, look! Look at the *big dogs*!"

I pull over and Riley stands to look out the open window and regard the cows. He wags his tail slowly.

"Let's see if they'll let him sniff them," Renie says.

"We've gone seventeen miles," I say. "Do you really think we should stop again already?"

"Stopping for gas doesn't count," Joni says.

Renie says, "And then after this, I need to pee."

"I told you not to get that huge-size coffee at the gas station!" Lise says. She snaps on Riley's leash.

"Oh, okay, I won't," Renie says and takes Riley's leash from Lise. "I'll take him. You won't let him get close enough."

"Don't let him get hurt," Lise says. "He's an old dog. Be careful. Don't let him get hurt."

"They're not *bulls*," Renie says. She brings Riley over to the fence and he takes a leisurely pee, pointedly facing away from the cows. Then he walks over to the one nearest him, his tail low and still.

"Riley, this is Elsie the cow," Renie says.

Elsie lowers her head and Riley sniffs her, then licks her nose. The cow's head jerks up and Lise leans out the window to say, "Okay, that's enough, back in the car. Come on."

Renie turns around. "How about if I just take his leash off and let him stampede a little bit?" But she gets back into the car, and after I pull onto the road, she says, "Seriously, though. About the burden thing? Some people have no more burden than an avocado going bad."

"That's not true!" I say, and so we pass the time until we come to a truck stop–type gas station, where Renie says she'll find some clothes and change in the ladies' room. The rest of us walk Riley. Again.

"I can't believe she walked into that store wearing pajamas," Joni says.

Lise shrugs. "Everybody wears pajamas outside now. When Sandy was in high school they had to ban kids showing up for class in their sleepwear."

"Yeah, well, Renie's not a kid," Joni says, and Lise says, "Oh?"

"I'M THE PERSON YOUR MOTHER WARNED YOU ABOUT?" Joni says, when Renie gets back in the car, about what's emblazoned across the front of the T-shirt she's wearing over a pair of surprisingly not-bad jeans.

Renie shrugs. "It was this or HOW CAN I LOVE YOU IF YOU WON'T LIE DOWN?"

"See, you're just being provocative right off the bat," Lise says. "This is how you get when you're scared."

"What?" Renie says. I tell her I've got a plain white blouse and a black blazer she can wear, and she goes back inside to change. I'm nervous for her. I wish she wasn't the first stop. I wish I could know that her daughter would show up and give her a chance. But I suppose that's what this journey is about for all of us: finding out.

ABOUT TEN MINUTES outside of Winona, there's a sign for home-made pie. It's tacked onto a rural mailbox in shaky handwriting. "Ohhhhh, look, look, look, look!" Joni says. "Let's go!"

I pull into the driveway and Renie says, "No, no, don't stop. We have to get there."

I look at my watch. "We practically are there. And it's only ten-forty."

"Too close," Renie says. "These roads aren't nearly as fast as the freeway. And what if we run into a train crossing? Plus I have to buy a rose. And I have to comb my hair and put on some . . . I don't know, ChapStick. I have to get centered, take a walk by myself, I'll take a walk before I go in. I have to calm down. I really have to calm down and think about what I want to say to her, I have to get *ready,* you guys, come on!" She sighs. "Sorry." She closes her eyes, rubs her forehead. "I'm obviously . . . Sorry."

"It's *homemade pie,*" Joni says. "Let's at least see if she makes her own crust. I'll bet she does. I'll bet she puts vinegar in it, too."

"Okay, listen," Renie says. "Why don't you drop me off and then come back? And then you can spend as much time as you like with Betty Crocker. You can come and get me anytime after one o'clock. I'll just wait for you."

Joni looks up at the house. "Let me just see what kinds she has. Would that be okay?"

"Can we just *go?*" Renie says.

"All right, but remember where this place is," Joni says. "We're coming back. "

"Isn't there a way to bookmark it or something on your GPS?" Lise asks.

"I'll remember where it is," I say. "Although I guess I could figure out how to do it. It might be this button. Or no, wait, I think it's—"

"*Go!*" Renie says, and I do.

We ride mostly in silence to the café, and I pull over to the curb about half a block away from it. Renie gets out of the car, straightens her blouse, tucks the yellow rose she swiped from someone's garden beneath her blazer. It was a crime mitigated by the fact that she left a five-dollar bill in the mailbox.

Not one of us says "Good luck," or anything else for that matter;

but I can feel the hope we all have for this to go well. Renie walks quickly away from us, turns back and waves, smiles, and goes on.

"Oh, this is awful," Lise says. "It's like your first kid's first day at school. I'm so anxious. I think I need a beta-blocker."

"Have mercy on her, Haley," Joni says. "Give her a chance."

"Amen," I say.

BETTY CROCKER IS a man. After we knock on the door, it's opened by a tall, hefty guy, maybe early eighties, wearing a T-shirt, baggy pants, suspenders, and brown leather slippers that have seen their better days. He has what looks like a few days' growth of white stubble on his face. He stares at the three of us standing there and finally says, "What do youse want?" His upper torso jerks when he speaks, as though someone's pulled the string to make him talk.

Joni says, "Pies?"

He leans in closer, cups a hand around one ear. "What's that?"

"Pies!" Joni says, louder.

"What about 'em?"

"You have a sign on your mailbox saying HOMEMADE PIES," I say.

"So what?"

Lise begins to laugh, but stops herself. She says loudly, "So we thought you sold homemade pies."

He straightens. "Youse going to buy some? I ain't got time otherwise."

"Well, we'd like to see them, first," Joni says.

"Ain't nothing to see, they're pie, only littler. Little pies. You want 'em or not?"

"I guess not," I say, and start to leave, but Joni takes my arm.

She steps closer to the man. "What kind you got?"

"What kind you want?"

"What kind you got?"

Lise and I look at each other. "I think we should go," she says, low.

"Oh, I got what you want," the man says. "Don't you worry about it."

"Okay, that's it," I say, and take off toward the car, Lise behind me.

But Joni stays. "How about apple?" we hear her say, and we turn around, waiting.

"Stay right there," the man says, and he comes back with a small pie that he hands Joni.

She smells it. "How much is it?"

"How much you want to pay?" the man asks.

"Three dollars," Joni says.

"Three dollars it is."

Joni opens her purse and Lise puts her hands over her mouth and says, "Oh no, don't open your purse, don't open your purse."

But the man stands there and does nothing until Joni hands him three dollars. Then he gives her back one. She turns to look at the two of us, poised for flight, and makes a face I can't decipher. No one says anything. Joni turns back to the man and says, "About your crust."

"What about it?"

"What do you put in it?"

"I put in it what needs to be in it."

"Flour, sugar . . ." Joni says.

"Yeah, course."

"Vinegar?"

"Course."

"Butter?"

"Nah. Don't need no butter."

Joni nods. "Lard, then. Do you put lard in? I'll bet you put lard in."

"What are you, a reporter?"

"I'm a chef."

The man stands there. Blinks. "Then what the hell are you doing buying a pie from me? Whyn't you make your own?"

"We're on a road trip," Joni says. She points to Lise and me. "All of us."

"Where youse going?"

"To see people from our past," Joni says.

"That so."

"That's so."

"Well, I might could give youse some more pies, then. Keep in the car, might get hungry."

"Do you have any blueberry?"

"No. But I got some pecan 'bout lay you out flat."

"We'll take a few."

The man smiles. "All right. Come on in."

And Joni goes in. So what can we do? We follow her.

WE GET BACK TO the café at one after one. Renie is standing outside, holding the blazer. Her face is determinedly neutral. Joni, who is driving, pulls into a parking place across the street, beeps the horn, and Renie comes running over. She gets into the back and snaps her seat belt on. "Next stop," she says.

Silence, and then I turn around and say, "So . . . ?"

Nothing.

Lise, sitting with arm around Riley's neck, gives me a look that says, *Don't push.*

Then Renie says, "You know what, it wasn't a good idea. But hey, I got something out of it. If someone writes to me now about whether or not to see the kid they gave up at birth, I'll know what to do. I'll say, 'Either that or shove toothpicks under your nails. One by one. Slowly.'"

"What happened?" Lise asks.

"On to Cleveland!" Renie says.

"Des Moines," Lise says, quietly.

"What?"

"It's Des Moines," Lise says. "That's the next stop."

"Oh. Right. Okay, then, on to Des Moines!"

"Okay," Joni says. "But can I just run in that café and pee?"

"Sure," Renie says. "They have great sandwiches. Also a great bathroom. I visited it a few times. That's mostly what I did. I sat at the table with really good posture and I went back and forth to the bathroom."

"Did she come?" I ask.

"Oh, yes," Renie says. "She was there the whole time, watching me. Then at about five of one, she dropped a note on my table and walked out. Yup. Dropped a note, gave me a look you might call withering, and walked out. She's quite pretty. Really pretty girl, big brown eyes, heart-shaped face. Tall."

"Read us the note," Joni says.

"Can't. I threw it away. It was mostly just her talking about what nerve I had, coming here and acting like we'd just pick up like old friends. Oh, and how stupid the rose was."

"Oh, Renie," I say.

"It doesn't matter," she says. "It was just a goof, really, I just wanted . . ."

But then her face falls and Lise moves closer to her, puts her arm around her. Joni pulls out of the parking place and starts to drive off, and a young woman comes running up behind us, yelling *"Wait! Wait! Hey! WAIT!"*

Joni stops the car and Renie undoes her seat belt.

"That's your daughter, all right," Lise says.

"I'll be right back," Renie says. "Go and get some lunch, I'll be right back."

Joni pulls back into the parking place and tells Renie, "Take as long as you want."

The girl *is* pretty. And I'm so glad she came back. I watch Renie walk up to her and say something, and the girl nods. Then they walk off together. Renie's head is down, her hands in her pockets; she's listening.

"I'm getting the sandwich that takes the most time to make," I say.

"I'm going to tell them to make the bread first," Joni says.

None of us is hungry. We all ate pie for lunch, courtesy of Mr. Brooks Daniels, who turned out to be swell. He invited us in, put Chet Baker on his turntable, cleared a stack of books, magazines, and a coffee-stained *Farmer's Almanac* off his kitchen table, and sat us down to sample his wares. He made good pie, every single kind was really good. Eating it, I had one of those punches delivered to the solar plexus: Penny would have adored this place.

"Who all youse going to see?" Brooks asked, and Joni told him.

"It's not always a good idea, digging around in the past," he said. "I done that once. I went to see the girl who got away. And I remembered real soon why I let her get away."

"Well, then you knew," I said. "Then you could put it to rest."

He grabbed a toothpick from a ceramic cowboy-boot holder at the center of his table. It was on a lazy Susan, along with salt and pepper, soy sauce, honey, and many kinds of hot sauce, including one called Ass Whoopin' Red Neck.

"I wouldn't say I put it to rest," he said. "Nope. Oh, I knew we's never gon' get together after all. But how she used to be in them days still comes along and snatches me up, now and then. And ever' once in a while, I dream of her real strong. Suzanne."

He'd been staring out the window, saying all this; his voice had lost some vitality. But then he looked at Joni and spoke so loudly I jumped. "I'll tell you something. My wife was a better person by far. But I never did let my wife have all the real estate in my heart. And then after my wife died and I seen Suzanne, well, I learnt what a mistake I made, holding out from Estelle that way. She was a good and gentle soul, she deserved a far sight better'n I give her."

I scraped the last of the pecan pie from my plate and said, "You can't help loving who you love."

He looked over at me, and in that instant I saw the man he used to be, saw that he must have been quite handsome in his day. "Well, that was my question, you see. I believe I done my wife wrong, being stingy that way, and maybe there was something I could have done about it, but ain't nothing I can do about it now. Is the problem."

He pushed himself away from the table and went into the living room. He came back with a photograph he dusted with his sleeve before he showed us. "This is her," he said. "Long time ago."

"Your wife?" I asked.

"No. Suzanne." He took off the back of the frame and pulled out another photo. "This one here's my wife. I alternate."

"Ah," I said, and held back a smile. His wife had a kindness in her face, but Suzanne was a bombshell.

"On account of what's the difference now?" he asked. "I alternate, and that way I feel like I have some company coming in and out of here."

Joni looked at her watch and gasped. "Uh-oh, we've got to go and get our friend." She started to gather the plates, and Brooks took them from her hand. "Never mind that. But wait one second. You might want to order some pies from me sometime. I'd box 'em up good and drive 'em on up to you." From a kitchen drawer, he pulled out a paper napkin, wrote down his information. Same shaky writing as the sign outside. A worthy souvenir, if nothing else, I thought. "My card," he told Joni, handing her the napkin.

Now, in the café, the three of us seated at a table by the high windows, Lise says, "This trip is great already. I'm really very happily surprised. It's kind of like the Christmas I was ten years old and I got the thing I wanted that I *never* thought I'd get."

"Which was?" I ask.

"A BB gun."

"What did you do with it?" Joni asks.

"I *shot* stuff. Shot boys."

"Really?" I asked.

"I missed, every time. But yeah, I tried to shoot these boys who were always shooting birds."

"I'm sorry you missed," I say.

Beneath the table, I spy a wadded-up piece of paper. I hold it up to show the others. "What are the *chances*?"

"That might not be it," Lise says.

I uncrinkle the paper. "It *is* it." I start to read it aloud. But then the waitress comes and I put the note in my lap and order the first thing I see on the menu. Which is the ham hoagie. Which Riley will be very happy about. Speaking of the trip being like Christmas.

The waitress finishes taking our order and I turn again to reading the note:

Miss Browne,

I'm sitting across the room from you. I recognized you when you first came in, you didn't have to put a rose on the table and especially shove it to the edge, no one could miss it. Kind of a stupid idea, really. I was going to talk to you, but now I don't really want to. My mom thought it might be fine, but she also has always told me to go with my gut and my gut is sort of screaming at me to get out of here. It's embarrassing to think about even introducing myself to you and anyway, why should I put myself out for you at all? I've babysat for a lot of infants, and every time I do, I look into their eyes and I see such trust. I don't know how you could have done what you did. Okay, you didn't want me or you couldn't take care of me or whatever but you just gave me away and that was that. And now you're guilty or curious or something and you call and I'm supposed to come running. Which kind of pisses me off that that's exactly what I did. I don't think there's anything you can say to me that will make up for all those times I wondered what was wrong with me that you couldn't even be bothered to send a birthday card. Although you probably forgot when my birthday is. Anyway, I'm just going to go and would ask that you don't try to contact me again. You have your life and I have mine.

Haley

I look up.

"She's mean," Joni says.

Lise says, "She's hurt."

"She's both." I look at the note again. "I think I should keep this in case Renie ever wants it."

"Maybe," Joni says. "But don't give it to her now. Wow. I wonder what they're talking about."

Silence, while we all ponder that.

We take turns going to the bathroom, and then our food arrives. We all sit staring at it. And the next time the waitress comes, we ask her to wrap it to go. Across the street, I see Riley pull his head back in from the partially open window. Wait till he sees this.

We are on the way out to the car to wait for Renie when we see her coming down the block. She waves, smiling, and when she gets in the car, she says, "I'm going to come back and visit in a few weeks. I saw the outside of where she lives. It's nice. She has a window box. And she's like me, a little. I really think I can see myself in her. And . . . I guess that's all I want to say right now."

Renie drives, Lise is up front with her, and Riley, Joni, and I are in back. We fall quiet, listening to the radio and to the smooth-voiced woman on GPS saying things like "In *half* of a mile, *right* turn." Then Joni takes her seat belt off and lies down, resting her head on Riley's rump.

"Put your seat belt on," Lise tells her, and Joni, her eyes still closed, says, "They're dangerous."

"What?" I say.

"They're dangerous. That's what my Aunt Peg always said. She was a pistol. She lived to be one hundred and two and she never did wear a seat belt and she got in a wreck once and she didn't get hurt at all."

I cross my arms, look out the window at the scenery passing by: the budding trees, a string of identical brick houses with white wooden front porches, a strip mall with a coffee shop called Down with Ground. We pass an empty playground, swings moving in the wind as though ghost children are in them. I take my seat belt off, too.

"All right, both of you put those seat belts on," Lise says, not even turning around, and then, "If Renie has to stop this car . . ."

I put my belt on. Then, after a minute, Joni does, too, but she stays lying down, her head still on Riley's rump. As for Riley, his head is in my lap. I rest my head against the window and close my eyes. I think of Michael, and what I think of as the miracle that happened yesterday.

"So tomorrow's the day, huh?" Michael had said, after I'd come in and settled myself in the chair next to his bed.

"Yup. We're leaving at six A.M. Or so we say, anyway."

Outside the room, I saw a flash of someone rushing by.

"What's the first stop?"

"Depends," I said. It happened again, that flash. A woman. I thought it was Phoebe. I stood up, headed for the door.

"Let her in," Michael said.

I turned toward him. "What?"

"Let her in. But if I . . . All right, look. Let her in, but you stay. If I want you to go, I'll raise my right arm to scratch my head. If I want you to get rid of her, I'll raise my left arm."

"Okay," I said. "You're sure?"

He nodded. I flew out the door. I realized I'd been wanting so much for him to let her in. In the last couple of days, he'd told me more and more about her, how they had just gotten engaged when he was diagnosed with leukemia. How they had frozen sperm before he started treatment. How at first the treatment had seemed as though it was going to work, but then it didn't. How he then wanted to cut ties with Phoebe so that she could find someone else and not suffer any longer on his account. "But are you maybe changing your mind?" I'd asked him.

"No."

"Because if you are—"

"I said no!"

"Fine," I'd said, a little miffed.

I went into the hall and saw no one, so I started for the lobby. Knowing that I was leaving the next day, I wanted him to have someone he could really talk to. When the other volunteer, Karen Night, came to stay with him, he never talked. He slept. Probably because I wore him out, but also I thought he talked to me because he liked me. As I did him. I tried not to think about the fact that he might not be there when I got back from my trip, but it was a possibility.

I looked for Phoebe in the lobby; no sign. I wondered if he'd let me call her. Or if he would call her. I was deep in thought when I bumped into someone. Phoebe.

"Oh!" I said. "You're here!"

"I'm going," she said, color rising in her face. "Okay?"

"No. No, I was coming to get you. He wants to see you."

She stood still, eyes wide.

"Come with me, he wants to see you."

We moved to the wall, out of the way of a medication cart coming through. Phoebe said, "Who are you?"

"My name is Cece Ross, and I'm a volunteer. I've just been sitting with Michael every day, just to talk, and—"

"And to watch for me," she said, though it was without rancor.

"Well, yes. But he wants to see you now."

"He does?"

"Yes."

"Are you sure?"

"He just now asked for you to come."

She nodded.

Together, we walked down the hall and into Michael's room. I went to the chair in the corner and sat. Phoebe moved slowly to the bedside, clutching her purse to her middle. "Michael," she said, and her voice cracked. She began to cry, hard, dropped her purse and put her hands over her face. Michael raised his right arm to scratch his head. And I could not for the life of me remember if I was supposed to stay or leave when he did that. I stood, pointed to myself, then to the door, with my eyebrows raised. *Go?* He nodded solemnly.

I walked out quietly, closing the door behind me.

I went to Annie's office and found her on the phone. She held up a finger and I stood before her. "May I call you right back?" Annie said and hung up. Then, to me, "What happened?"

"Phoebe's with Michael."

Annie jumped up out of her chair, and I said, "No, he wants her to be."

"Oh!" She sat back down. "Oh, I'm so glad."

"Me, too."

"And on your last day!"

"Yes."

"You will come back after your trip, won't you?"

"Of course. I'll go through the whole training then."

She smiled. "Good. We'll be glad to have you." She looked toward the front door, where a dark-haired woman was being wheeled in, a number of people in attendance, a few of them weeping. "I have to go and admit someone," she said. "Have a wonderful time on your trip. It's going to be so much fun!"

I thought of that famous Savannah cemetery statue, the one of the woman holding a plate in each hand, balancing them perfectly. That's who Annie reminded me of. I thought of how much I admire people who are able to not let one side of life cancel out the other, who can face up to opposing sides of it fully, often at the same time.

I walked home, thinking about Michael, wondering what he and Phoebe were talking about. My third day there, I'd read him some haiku, and we'd talked about how much we both liked it, the simplicity of the form. I'd made one up on the spot, a silly one about robins and their blue eggs. And then he'd made one up:

> *On a windy day*
> *Her hair lifts and my heart breaks*
> *And that was before*

After a moment, I'd said, "That's lovely." And then, "Phoebe?" He'd shrugged.

I'd known enough not to say any more.

I hope she's with him now, as close to him as she can be.

I listen to the hypnotic sound of the tires on the road, and feel myself falling asleep.

When I awaken, Lise and Joni are talking about people they were mean to in high school. "Patricia Gunderson," I say, my eyes still closed. "Everybody was mean to her, she was the it girl for meandom. She wore black cat-eye glasses with rhinestones. She wore sweater guards and white ankle socks, and she had a voice like a foghorn. She carried a bucket purse with two rabbits' feet, pink ones. She had really frizzy hair and she wore velvet bow barrettes on either side of her head every day. She drank coffee at lunch and her only friends were teachers. She's probably some famous artist who lives in Portland now and does interviews about her dopey classmates who had no idea how ahead of her time she was."

"Do you wish you could apologize to her?" Joni asks.

I open my eyes and look down at her. "Yes. Maybe. Yeah, I would. I would like to say, 'Patricia, I just want to say I'm sorry for being so mean to you in high school. Although I wasn't the meanest, I think you'll agree, I think you'll agree that Annie Whitmore was the meanest.' "

"And what do you think Patricia would say?" Lise asks.

I shrug. "I don't know. Probably, 'Who are you?' "

Lise turns up the radio for "Long Cool Woman in à Black Dress."

After the song finishes, she says, "That's one of those songs that, if it comes on when you're driving around, you just feel *hot.*"

Renie, her mouth full of red licorice, points out the window. "Rook! A chatu parror!" She turns into the strip mall, where there's a tattoo parlor.

"You're getting a tattoo?" I ask.

"I am!"

Frankly, I'm surprised she doesn't have one already. She parks in front of Branded! and turns off the engine.

Lise says, "I don't know, Renie. It doesn't look all that clean."

But Renie's out of the car and on her way in.

Lise turns around to look at me and Joni. "It doesn't look *clean.*"

"Well, let's just go in," I say. "Maybe it's better on the inside."

"Yeah, and maybe it's worse," Lise says.

"I might get one," Joni says, shyly. "Just on my ankle. A little bitty one. Maybe just my initials or a butterfly."

"Oh, please," Lise says. She looks at me. "Are you going to get one, too?"

"Not on your life."

"Fine, you can sit with me and read magazines. They probably have *Modern Mercenary.*"

We go inside. The place is dim, but not really dirty. There's a black tile floor, fluorescent lighting, and the walls are painted red. New age music is playing, which really surprises me. I suppose the guy doing the artwork wants to keep calm.

There are three chairs with armrests, big comfortable things that look like what you sit in to give blood, and a couple of straight-back chairs along the wall. Renie is standing by one of the big chairs where an overweight, heavily tattooed man with multiple face studs is sitting on a stool and holding a tattoo gun, apparently getting ready to work on his client, a hypermuscular young man who looks to be in his twenties. The client is draped, and his arm, which already has tattoos, shines with some sort of preparation the big guy has just sprayed on him. The big guy is wearing a black plastic apron over a black shirt and black jeans. And now he snaps on black vinyl gloves.

"Hey," he says. "Y'all want tattoos, too? Getting busy!"

"No, we're just waiting for her," I say, gesturing toward Renie.

"I might want one," Joni says. "Just a little one."

"Well, we got those," the guy says. "Got a lot of real pretty little ones. Flowers and birds and such. I'm Eddie, by the way. Y'all have a look at the sample books we got, we got pictures of everything we do. Y'all like sunsets? They're my favorite to do. Course they take a long time, a few hours."

"I think I just want a little butterfly," Joni says.

"That don't take no time at all," Eddie says. "I can have you on your way in 'bout half an hour."

He turns his attention to Renie. "Okay, so you ready?" He tells us,

"Your friend wanted to see one done 'fore she decides for sure. Gon' watch Michelangelo at work here!"

He turns on his tattoo gun, and a horrible sound fills the air. It's like a dentist's drill, only worse. He starts drawing on the client's arm.

"How long does it take to heal?" Renie asks. Shouts.

"'Bout two weeks," Eddie says. "And you can't be touching it with a towel or nothing like that."

"Does it hurt?" Renie asks the guy who's getting the tattoo.

He shrugs. "It's just like a hot scratch. No biggie."

The tattoo gun whines and whines.

"Okay, I'm just going to wait outside," I say.

"I think we'll go and get some ice cream," Lise says.

"I'm coming," Joni says.

"Don't you want your little butterfly?" the guy asks, and Joni says, "No, thank you."

"Hold up," Renie says, and the guy says, "Aw, come on, you're leaving, too?"

"I'd love to do it, but I didn't realize how much time it took. We're on a trip and . . . I gotta go."

She walks quickly over to join us and we go outside.

"What were you going to get?" Joni asks Renie.

"I kind of liked the little fairy kneeling coyly in the flowers," Renie said. "But then there was also the viper with his mouth wide open. My favorite, though, was the woman dressed in a black leather bra and panties and black nylons, straddling a giant tongue. I had one all picked out for each of the rest of you, too. Lise was going to get a caduceus on her deltoid; Joni was going to get a pineapple on her ankle; and for you, Cece? A pithy aphorism, just above your sacrum, in Angelina Jolie script."

"Seriously, do you really want a tattoo?" I ask.

"Not anymore," Renie says. She climbs into the back of the car and slams the door. "Somebody else drive."

"I think it looked a little like hell in there," Joni says. "Did anybody else think it looked like hell in there? Those red walls, and all that black."

"They had a devil tattoo," Renie says. "Also a Jesus and a Buddha one. Never let it be said that they aren't open-minded in hell."

"Has anyone ever been to Des Moines?" Lise asks, buckling herself into the driver's seat. She's told the others about her plans to go there and see her ex-husband.

It's quiet in the car, so I guess not.

"If I would have predicted what I'd be doing at forty-two years old, I would never have said I'd be on a road trip to see my ex-husband. In Des Moines, of all places."

"What do you mean, *of all places*?" Joni says.

"I don't know," Lise says. "Des Moines just sounds like a city that you would use in a joke or something, like New Jersey."

"You're a snob," Joni says.

"The original name for Des Moines was Fort Raccoon," I say, helpfully.

"How do you know?" Renie asks.

"Fourth grade, Mrs. Menafee. We had to learn interesting things about cities and I got Des Moines. It also has the largest gold dome in North America, on the state capitol."

"See?" Lise says. "That's not interesting. If that's all you can—"

"Every place is interesting if you open your eyes," I say.

"That's so bumper sticker," Lise says.

"It's true!"

"She tried to find me a few times," Renie says, and it appears we're on to another subject.

"Haley?" Lise says.

"Yeah."

"Why didn't she find you? Everybody's findable these days. *Santa Claus* has two websites."

"I don't know. That's just what she said. That she tried."

"What's she like?" I ask.

"Well, the reason I said she's like me is that she's guarded, like I can be. Even after she came back, she was pretty defensive, but then I expected that. Mostly we just kept sneaking looks at each other, and a lot of the content of what we said was lost to that. You know: Oh my God, it's my *mother*, oh my God, it's my *daughter*. I did, you know, apologize, after a fashion. And she accepted it, after a fashion. It went like this: I said there was a lot I'd like to explain to her about the circumstances of her birth. And she said she'd like to hear about that sometime. So."

"So did you really feel like you were her mother?" Joni asks.

"I don't know. I felt something. What does it feel like to be a mother?"

Quiet, and then Joni says, "You know those doors where you go in and you can't come out?"

"What doors can you go in and not come out?" Renie asks.

"They're in mousetraps."

"Being a mother feels like being in a mousetrap?" Renie asks, laughing.

"A *humane* one," Joni says. "You're trapped because you're always on call. Even when they get older, they still need you."

Lise's cellphone rings. *Sandy,* she mouths, and starts talking to her daughter about how to use the washer. Now that Lise isn't there, Sandy has deigned to pay a visit.

"They especially need you when you're not there," Joni says.

"Thanks a lot," Renie says.

"I didn't mean . . . I just meant that . . . Look how Sandy has called Lise twice on this trip, and you know she never calls her."

"Yes she does," Renie says. And then, after a moment, "Yeah. You're right, she never does."

"We're not too far from Des Moines," Lise says, into the phone. "And we're having a great time."

We. It's good to have friends, that fleshy stockade.

Lise sighs. "Nothing! I'd just like to see him again. It's been a long time. Cece is seeing someone she hasn't seen for—"

She listens, then says, "Okay, you know what, Sandy? You're getting way ahead of—"

She listens again. "No. No I'm *not.* Will you just . . . All right, look. I'll talk to you later."

She hangs up.

Silence, and then Renie asks to have the radio turned up.

Lise adjusts herself in a way that looks like she's either casting something off or readjusting it so that it will hang better on her.

"Good store, good store!" Joni yells, pointing to a cooking store called Pannifed, and we all pitch forward when the brakes are put on.

When we come out, Lise is bitching that all the new pots Joni bought won't fit in the kitchen and Joni is bitching that Lise bought a coffee press that is the wrong kind. Renie bought polka-dot coffee mugs, a variety of fancy salts, and almond-scented dish detergent.

I. Bought. Nothing.

LISE AND I ARE SHARING A ROOM AT THE MOTEL IN DES MOINES. I'm waiting for her to finish getting ready to see Steven. She comes out of the bathroom dressed in a blue sheath dress and a string of pearls, her usual pearl studs. Low, bone-colored heels.

She sits on the edge of the bed, her hands tightly clasped, looks at her watch.

"Ten minutes."

"Uh-huh."

"My heart rate is one-sixty."

"You look really nice."

It's as if those words launch her back into the bathroom. She comes out in a couple of minutes changed into a pair of black pants, a plain white button-down, sandals. The necklace is off.

She sits back down on the bed and looks over at me. "Better, I think."

"You looked lovely in that dress. Was it new?"

"Well, that's right. That's part of the problem. I want to be comfortable, and I can't be comfortable in a new dress. Or . . . in a dress period. Better to be comfortable."

"You still look nice."

"Thanks. Cece, will you wait outside with me for him to come?"

"Of course."

"It's a gray Avalon we'll be looking for. Help me to look for a gray Avalon."

"I will."

"Do you know where Renie and Joni are? I don't want them to come out there. I don't want it to be . . . a spectacle."

"They went to the pool. They said they were going to have a soak in the hot tub."

Lise nods. "I wish that's where I was going."

I reach over to touch her hand. "You'll be fine. You need to do this. The cards said it would be good."

"They didn't say that."

"Well, they didn't say it would be bad."

She looks at her watch. "Okay. Five minutes of. Let's go."

We go down to the lobby, and she looks out the window. "Oh God, he's here." She looks over at me. "I shouldn't have done this."

"Just . . . Have a good time. Have a good time! We'll see you later."

She goes out toward the car, and a tall, silver-haired man gets out to open the door for her. He's good-looking, from what I can tell from here. He closes the door and goes around to his own side, and I see Lise make the tiniest wave at me. I wave back, then go and change into my bathing suit. It doesn't matter how old I am, it doesn't matter how I look in a suit (though this black halter-top one was designed by a compassionate person and I really like it). Putting on a bathing suit always gets me a little jazzed; I'm ready to have a good time. I cannot remember ever having a bad time in a bathing suit. I think about this in the elevator, on the way down to the pool, and it's really true, I haven't.

———

JONI, RENIE, AND I are back in the hot tub after having gone out to Dairy Queen, where we had sundaes and onion rings for dinner. A young couple comes into the pool room in their bathrobes. They stand a few feet away from the hot tub, watching, then leave the room. Almost immediately, though, the young man comes back and says, "Are you going to be in there much longer?"

"We just got in," Joni says. "But there's room for you two, if you want." She gestures, in a halfhearted kind of way, to the other side of the hot tub, where there is indeed room for two more people.

"That's okay," he says, and leaves again.

But now the woman comes in and walks over to the edge of the hot tub and crouches down beside us. "Could I just tell you something?"

"Sure," I say.

"We just got married? And we wanted to sort of have the hot tub to ourselves?" She's a pretty girl, an open-faced blonde with a well-placed beauty mark above her lip. Her husband, too, is a fine specimen, though a little on the blank-eyed side.

I start to climb out and Renie yanks on my arm to pull me back down.

"I so know what you mean?" Renie says. "But we got here first? And you'll just have to wait your turn? To have sex in the hot tub?"

"Renie!" I say.

"What?"

"They're not going to have sex in the hot tub!"

"Yes, we are," the girl says, giggling.

"We'll be out in just a few minutes," I say.

"Or whenever we feel like it," Renie calls after the girl as she walks away.

"Age before sex," she tells me.

"People have sex in public hot tubs?" I ask.

"Duh," Joni says.

"Really?" I start to lift myself out.

"Oh, if you only knew," Joni says. "But don't worry, they put stuff in the water to kill *everything*."

I hang there, half in the water, half out. Part of me is thinking, *Oh, relax. It's too late now. Whatever is in here is in you already.* I sit back down.

A few minutes later, the door to the pool room bangs open and here comes Lise. I can't read her face.

She pulls a chair up to the edge of the hot tub, slides her sandals off, and sticks her feet in.

Nobody says a word and then she says, "Well, *this* was a bad idea."

"Was he a jerk?" Renie asks.

Lise shakes her head no.

We wait, and finally she says, "He was wonderful. I'd forgotten how witty he is, how smart. I'd forgotten that he was such a bad tipper, too; I slipped some cash on the table when we were leaving. How can you not tip on the whole bill? How can you exclude the alcohol? Especially when you're making a ton of money; he's making a ton of money."

"But what happened?" Joni asks. "What else happened?"

"I'm going to tell you. But first I'm wondering if I should go and put on my bathing suit."

"It is really nice in here," I say.

"Don't go and put on your suit!" Renie says. "Tell us what happened!"

Lise sits still for a moment, trying to decide what to do. Then she rolls up her pants legs neatly and puts her legs in farther. "So," she says. "He's the same, but he's different. He's . . . Well, he's grown up, I guess you'd say. As have I. And I . . ." She looks at me. "Oh God. I really like him. I like him again."

"Uh-oh," Renie says.

"We went to his house after dinner and he put on a really nice Thelonious Monk CD. I asked him when he had gotten into Monk. He said he had always loved Monk, I just hadn't known because I'd never asked. His house was nice: earthy colors, comfortable furniture. I saw a picture of Sandy and at first it was so jarring. I thought, *What is he doing with a picture of my daughter?* And then I realized, of course, that she was his daughter, too. And that just seemed so cozy and convenient and *nice.*

"We had a really good talk about her and he said he had no idea she was so awful to me, that in fact she spoke very well of me when she was around him. And when I went into his bedroom I saw a framed note on his dresser from Sandy saying she was sorry, he was right, and I realized that she must give him a hard time, too. But apparently he's able to have a sense of humor about it, a necessary perspective. I realized I need to do that, too. And he is the perfect one to show me how."

"His bedroom, huh?" I say.

She smiles. "He had this huge bouquet of flowers on his dining room table, and he said he'd gotten those for me, did I still like roses? I said, 'So you figured we'd come back to your place, huh?' and he said he'd only hoped for it. And then he put his hand alongside my face and I . . . Well, I started crying. And he kissed me, and we . . . Anyway.

"Afterward—"

"Wait a minute, wait a minute!" Joni says. "What came before afterward?"

"*Afterward,*" Lise says, "we had a really good conversation. Really honest. And we both admitted to some flaws we'd never admitted to before. I admitted to my . . . Well, I can be uptight. Sometimes I'm a little uptight."

"*You?*" Renie says, mockingly.

"I can be looser, though," Lise says. "If I want to." She looks around the room, then back at us. "Watch this," she says, and slides fully into the hot tub.

"Huh?" she says, and spreads her arms expansively along the sides of the tub.

"Great," Renie says. "You got wet with your clothes on. Very wild. Now tell us more about what *happened.*"

"Okay. I'll just say it: I think he might move back to Minneapolis."

A stunned silence. Then everyone starts talking at once.

WANT TO HAVE BREAKFAST AT A TRUCK STOP, AND I THINK LISE will probably complain, she of the Teutonic attitude toward healthy eating—she's a big reason Joni got started with really healthy cooking—but she doesn't say a word about the prospect. She says, "Oh, that might be fun."

"I'm having biscuits and gravy," I say, to make sure she's really listening.

We're just getting in the car when my cellphone rings. I see that the call is from the Arms. *Annie,* I think. *Something has happened to Michael.*

"I'll be right back," I say, climbing out of the car and walking a distance away.

But it's not Annie calling, it's Michael, saying, "I got your number from Annie, I hope you don't mind."

"Of course not."

"Are you having fun?"

"Yes! It's even better than I thought it would be."

His voice lowers. "So, I need to ask you something. When exactly are you coming back?"

I estimate the date, then say, as casually as I can, "Why?"

"Just wanted to know," he says.

I hesitate, then go ahead and ask. "How are you, Michael?"

"The same. Nothing new. Hanging on. But Phoebe is here every day now. That's new. She's here every day."

"Is that good?"

The silence on the other end lasts so long I finally say, "Hello?"

"Yeah, it's good," he says, and then, briskly, "Okay, come and see me as soon as you can after you get back."

Lise toots the horn and I hold a finger up to her, *Wait.*

"I'll come right away," I say. "I won't even unpack."

"You can unpack," he says, and I tell him I hate unpacking and welcome any excuse not to.

When I get back in the car I hear Joni ask Lise, "So is he a good kisser?"

"Yes, he is, he always was, but you know what the best thing was? We were finishing dinner and he all of a sudden got up out of his chair and came over and planted a kiss right on the top of my head. And then he said, 'There, I'm sorry; I just had to do that,' and sat back down and smoothed his tie, and I'd forgotten how much I love that gesture, a man smoothing his tie down. I pushed my plate away and said, 'Let's go.'"

"Is he really thinking about moving to Minneapolis?" Renie asks. "Or was that the martini talking?"

"It was the martini talking," Lise says. "But also I think he might move to Minneapolis. Not just because of me; he was already thinking about taking a job offer there. And he'd be closer to Sandy."

"So, do you want him to?" I ask. "I mean, here in the cold light of day?"

She looks over at me and her face grows serious. "I don't know. I had a dream a couple of days before we left. It was about Steve, and we were standing out on the front porch and I was holding him really tight. I was just sobbing. I was saying *I was a terrible wife, I was so terrible, but if you would just come home.* I could feel him shaking; he was crying, too. He was dressed all in black, and it was shiny, like a costume. He had brought an empty shopping cart with him, and it was parked at an angle on the lawn like a car for sale. After I begged him to come home, he pulled away from me and grabbed his cart and put a magician's hat on and walked away.

"That dream means you can't trust him," Renie says. "He's a trickster."

"It means he is no longer going to deceive you," I say.

"What do you think, Joni?" Lise asks.

"I don't know. I think it was a dream. What matters is what *you* think. When you're *awake.*"

Silence, then, as the car pulls into the gravel lot of the truck stop. We all get out and walk quickly to the entrance. This is a good truck stop restaurant, it's not a chain, or at least none of us have ever heard of it. There are roosters everywhere: an exuberant one on top of the restaurant with his wings unfurled and his open beak pointed skyward, figurines along the windowsills, even the wallpaper features roosters. The place is called Doodle Doo's, and I think if you were having a bad day and a friend called and said "Do you want to go and get some eggs at Doodle Doo's?" a lot of that bad energy would immediately disappear.

When we sit at the booth and are handed menus, it takes Renie one second to decide. "I'm getting the Long Haul," she says.

I read the description: three eggs, three strips of bacon, three sausages, two biscuits and gravy, grits, large orange juice, and a bottomless cup of coffee.

"Order the same thing for me," Lise says, and heads off to the bathroom.

"Did she say to order the same thing for her?" Renie asks.

"Maybe she doesn't know what you got," I say. "She was in a big hurry to get to the bathroom."

"I'll bet she's going to email him," Renie says. Then, to me, she says, "While you were on the phone, she checked her email and there was one from him but she wouldn't tell us what he said."

The waitress, a tired-looking brunette with a thin ponytail and the smallest waist I've seen since Dolly Parton, takes our order and then we take turns guessing whether or not what he said was romantic, sexual, or funny.

"Funny is best," Renie says, and Joni says, "Yeah, but she didn't laugh. Or share it with us. So I think it was romantic. And you know what? I hope she lets whatever might happen, happen. I hope she won't let Sandy dictate what she should do."

"Sandy's just scared of getting hurt again, don't you think?" I say. "We were talking about it last night and Lise wondered if she and Steve had changed enough to give it another go, or if it might mess things up even more with Sandy. There'd be an awful lot of pressure on them to succeed."

"Too bad you didn't bring your box," Joni says, and I look over at her, smiling.

"Really?" she says. "You brought it?"

"I brought my favorite deck of cards. Just in case."

"Let's do them tonight!" Joni says. "There's something I want an opinion on."

"Lise should have a secret relationship with Steve for a while," Renie says. "Seems to me it's started already."

When Lise slides back into the booth, Joni says, "So?"

"What?" Lise's eyes are big.

"Oh, come on, tell us."

She smiles, then pulls out her phone, calls up the message, and reads it to us: *"It seems to me that you still have that same way about you, a sweetness, a kindness, and a vulnerability, but also a chronic and tightfisted resistance to things that might in fact be very good for you. My goal, if I may have one as pertains to you, is to convince you that I still want all of you, and think maybe we can rebuild a life together. I know how important it is for us to regain trust. I suppose some may find it miraculous that my feelings for you remain, especially when you made it so painfully clear all those years ago that you were not in the least bit interested in staying married to me. I confess it surprised me, the force with which so many things came back as soon as I saw your face. But you and I both know there's more to the human heart than anatomy and physiology taught us. Tell me honestly how you're feeling today, after a night that went a lot better than I think either of us suspected it would. Know that whatever you tell me is safe with me. Know, too, that I have no intention of moving back to Minneapolis this afternoon. But a visit soon with a walk around the lake might be nice. We always did like that."*

"Wow," Renie says. "What'd you say back?"

She shrugs. "I said, *'Come.'*"

The waitress bangs down our platters, and Lise looks at hers and says, "I ordered this?"

"You did," Renie says, her mouth already full.

"The biscuits and gravy are actually really good," Joni says.

Lise dives in. "I owe you," she tells me.

"For eating this?"

"For thinking of this trip."

"Oh. You're welcome."

"Don't you guys ever tell him I read you his email," Lise says.

Renie puts down her fork. "Damn it."

"What?" Lise says.

"Is he going to move in?"

"No! We're just . . . I don't know, Renie, we'll see. I'm a long way from living with him again."

Renie looks over at me. "When he moves in, you and I find another place, right?"

"What about me?" Joni asks.

"Oh," Renie says. "That's right. Well, I think the easiest thing is that Lise will have to move out." Satisfied, she resumes eating.

I dip my toast into the egg yolk, and think how odd it is, how odd and wonderful, that at any age, and all of a sudden, just the prospect of love can draw the curtains open to such a dazzling day.

Many years ago, I went to see a very famous novelist speak after her latest book had come out. It was in a huge auditorium that was packed with people. She was so eloquent, so clearly respected and admired, and beautiful to boot. She said many noteworthy things, thoughtful and really intelligent things. But you know what's stayed with me all these years? She was asked a question just before she left the stage, and she answered by saying, "Oh, well, I'm like everybody else: when it comes to love, I'm just a fool." And all of us sitting in the dark, thinking, *Oh, good. Oh, phew.*

After breakfast, I get into the driver's seat, adjust the mirrors, turn the key, back out of the lot, and head for wherever the freeway is not.

I watch the miles go past, and I think about whether Dennis and I could still be right for each other. If we could be right for each other long-term.

At the first bathroom break, I let the others go in before me, telling them I need to make a phone call. But after they've disappeared, I get out the cards. *How likely?* I ask. *How much of a chance do we have of ending up together, finally?*

I draw Cradleboard, "Ability to respond." I'm not supposed to sit and wait for someone else to do something. I'm supposed to use my creativity and speak my truth.

Well, that's a stupid card. All it does is fill me with fear. How am I supposed to use my creativity? What am I supposed to respond to? Maybe I shouldn't even be doing this. Maybe it's just too late. Although why should I think it's too late when my mother is currently starring in *The Housewives of HavenCrest*?

How can I calm down? I think, and draw another card. I get Whirling Rainbow, "Unity/Wholeness achieved." I'm being asked to remove discord in my life in order to grow. To not feed negativity. To create new beauty and abundance in my life.

I close the book, put it and the cards back in my tote.

All right. All right. I go into the gas station, where Renie is standing in front of gigantic ropes of beef jerky. "Want some?" she asks.

That night, Joni and I share a motel room and she asks to borrow my cards. She lies on her bed, closes her eyes, and pulls a card from the deck, then reads from the book. "This is really interesting," she says. "This is helping me make up my mind, all right."

"What's your question?"

"I can't tell you yet. I'll tell you at some point, but not yet. It's too . . . I have to be sure before I tell you."

"Well, what did you draw?"

"Whirling Rainbow," she says.

We're on a stretch of relatively uninteresting road in Indiana heading for Cleveland and Renie is working on her column. "Listen to this one," she says. "A woman who works at an airline ticket counter is complaining that passengers come to her and ask questions without saying 'Good morning' or 'How are you?' and she wants to know how to respond to such rude people."

"And . . . ?" I say.

"And here's what I've got so far. *'Thank you for asking this very important question. Here is what I'd suggest you say to the next beleaguered person who has waited in a slow-moving line of more than enough people to populate an incorporated town and dares to come up to you with a question pertaining to, oh, say, air travel rather than an inquiry as to how you are feeling at any particular time. I'd suggest you say, "Okay, where's my gift? You show up here with no gift? Go and get a gift and then get back in line."'*"

"Or," Lise says, "you could tell her to say, *'First, on behalf of my airline and myself, I'd like to apologize to you for whatever airline experience you just had or are about to have, because it isn't going to be good. Now let me see if I can help you with your question. If I can't, I'll probably take it out on you.'*"

"I feel sorry for airline employees," I say, and Joni says, "Me, too."

"Look!" Renie says, pointing. "A Carnegie library! Let's go in and all of us find a good quote. And then let's eat."

As we're getting out of the car, Lise says, "I might start making art boxes," apropos of nothing.

"What do you mean?" I ask.

"You know, sort of like Cornell boxes, only deeply personal. I might start making those."

"When did you start thinking of doing that?" Joni asks.

"Last night, Steve reminded me that I used to talk about that before we were married. We had seen an exhibit where a woman used old purses to create dioramas, and I felt so drawn by the notion of doing that kind of thing. I wanted to try doing it, using common objects in a very different way. What if this trip changes my life and all I want to do is make art boxes? What if there's a whole different me under the me I know?"

It seems possible. Already I've seen that when you're pulled away from your normal routine, it's as though air and sunlight come into your brain and do a little housecleaning. A lifting up of what's been practically rusted into place to reveal something else, a thing that makes you understand the origin of the phrase *new and exciting,* a phrase usually offered with irony, in order to hide the longing.

We go into the library, that layman's priory, that paper-scented oasis of quiet industry and calm. I wander around the place to admire the graceful architecture and to pull books off the shelf to read a little here, a little there. It's going to be hard to find a good quote, because every book says the same thing: *Dennis, Cleveland, tomorrow; Dennis, Cleveland, tomorrow.*

———

WE ARE AT a roadside restaurant that I want to go to for dinner because of the name, Sunny's No Foolin' Home Cookin' Cafe. It looks like a house that's been converted into a restaurant, and when we walk in, we see that it hasn't been converted so very much. We are seated in what was a bedroom, which accommodates four small tables. I tell the others to order the meat loaf platter for me, and make my way to the bathroom, which is a bathroom like in a house, complete with tub and a crocheted cover for the extra roll of toilet paper.

When I return to the table, Renie is saying, "Well, I'm going to ask her."

"Ask what?" I say, sitting down.

"I'm going to ask the waitress if she thinks everyone is carrying a heavy burden."

"That again?"

"It's time to start my research. She'll tell me what she really thinks; I can tell."

When the waitress appears, I think Renie must be right. The woman is tall and muscular, blond going gray, with a direct gaze and a no-nonsense attitude. "You the meat loaf?" she asks, and I say yes, I am.

"Best thing on the menu," she says.

"I thought you said the broasted chicken was the best thing," Joni says.

"It is." She puts a platter of catfish in front of Renie. "That's the best thing, too." When she puts down Lise's chef salad, she says nothing.

"What, no good?" Lise says.

She shrugs. "It's a salad." She puts her hands on her hips. "All set, girls?"

"Before you go, let me ask you something," Renie says. "There's this saying, *Be kind, for everyone is carrying a heavy burden.* Do you think that's true?"

"Hell, no!" she says, and Renie's face says, *See?*

"I *was.* But I got rid of my burden, and I'm happy as I guess you get to be in this life. It took me thirty years, but I finally left a husband who it turns out couldn't wait for me to go. I left the stuck-up suburb we lived in, moved here and took this job, which is mostly just fun, and bought myself a trailer, which is much nicer than you might think. The thing that's most surprising is the closet in the bedroom; I'm going to tell you, this thing must have been designed by a woman. And I'll bet she was thinking, *What do you need with a bunch of crap in your bedroom? You need a bed and a dresser and a closet that earns its keep.* And that's what I got.

"My place is walking distance from here, over in Arrowhead Court, you can see my trailer if you want. I get off in twenty minutes."

We look at each other, and she says, "Talk amongst yourselves and decide. Makes me no nevermind. I wouldn't mind having a little company tonight. If it's not you all, I'll find me somebody else."

She goes out of the room and Renie whispers, "Want to go?" and we all nod.

Forty minutes later, we're in Wanda's living room, three of us lined up on a gold sofa, Renie in one of the two swivel club chairs, also gold. We've been shown the closet, which is indeed impressive, and now Wanda takes a pack of cigarettes from a drawer in the table by her chair. "Cigarette?" she asks Renie, and Renie takes one. We all do. After a moment, Renie says, "This isn't tobacco."

Wanda looks over at her, a mirthful glance. "It isn't?" She leans back in her chair, looks at Renie. "So let me ask you something. How come you asked me if I was carrying a heavy burden? Do I look like I am?"

"No, it's just a goof," Renie says.

"What do you mean?"

"A goof, you know, just a question I keep bringing up for the hell of it."

Wanda nods, then says, "I'll tell you, though. I do think all people carry one burden, and that's fear. It's a problem, what fear makes people do, and also what it keeps them from doing. I mean, it was fear kept me from doing with my life what I wanted to. And why? I didn't have any responsibilities to anyone but myself; wasn't going to hurt anybody by getting out of what I was in, and going in a new direction entirely. But fear, you know, the boogeyman under the bed, you're just scared of making a change. And then one day you just go ahead and do it anyway and there you are: blue skies."

She rises up out of her chair. "Anybody want some Cheez Doodles?"

She fills a bowl with them and sets it down where we can all reach it, then says, "Fear and lack of love, those are the A-number-one problems of human beings. Every time there's another disaster, you know, somebody shooting up a place, you look. Fear. And a lack of love. Or, you know, something wrong with the hard wiring, and they just couldn't take any love they were ever offered. Or ask for it."

She eats another Cheez Doodle. "Well, now I'm thirsty. Ain't that the way? You get one good thing, you just want more." She goes over to her little fridge and leans in. "Who wants a Dr Pepper or . . . a Dr Pepper?"

A chorus of *I dos*, and she hands us each a can. "You all been friends for a long time, huh?"

I smile. "Not so long, really."

"Huh. Well, there's an ease to you. I can see you're having fun."

"That we are," Lise says.

"Nothing like a pack of women, having fun," she says. And then, leaning forward, her elbows on her knees, "*Anything* can happen."

"WOW," JONI SAYS. "I never do stuff like this."

It's late, approaching midnight, and we're ready to find a motel, but first we are lying out in a field looking up at a sky that should have put flyers all over town to announce the show it would be giving tonight.

"I do it all the time," Renie says, and Joni says, "No you don't."

"Well, I *want* to do it all the time, and I *used* to."

"Boy, that's my theme song," I say.

It's very quiet, and then somebody snorts, laughing. And then I laugh. And then we all do, we lie in the dark under the stars laughing and laughing. For too long, really. And then Joni rolls up onto to her elbows and says, "I don't know why I'm laughing so hard."

"Because we can," Lise says, and she's right. It's as though there's a dome of power around us, four women lying on the night-cooled earth, looking up and giving props to the same sky Cro-Magnon saw. Though for him the constellations were even clearer, much clearer, I'm sure. But this is enough, this starscape and these women and this moment.

I think I know why Wanda thought we'd been friends for a long time. Because of fate, because of timing, because of our own blend of chemistry, and because of this trip, we do share that kind of friendship. We're ahead of where we should be. And I realize now that I've been gifted, if not by a replacement of Penny, then by some pretty fine compensation for her loss.

"Hey, Renie," I say, thinking of the day I met her. "We're lying outside and looking up at the stars and sharing our innermost *thoughts and feelings.*"

"Yeah. All we need is to hold hands," she says, but there's a softness in it. And when I pick up her hand and squeeze it, it takes her a minute to let go.

"ARE YOU NERVOUS?" JONI ASKS. I HAVE BEEN SITTING STIFF and silent as a mannequin for the last fifty miles. The day before we left, I'd sent Dennis a postcard telling him that I thought we'd arrive today, probably early evening. But because of our erratic route, we're going to be late. Today we stopped at a ramshackle building missing half its corrugated metal roof called Atlas Garage: Home of the Mighty Fixers; Vi's Pies, which were not as good as Brooks Daniels's, but a close second; the Museum of the Stamp, with its earnest curator; and we stopped to take photos of a sign for a small town announcing its population as NOT MANY.

I'd given Dennis my cellphone number again on that postcard, and he'd finally sent me his, a single entry on one of his photo postcards. I hoped that this simply reflected his disinterest in talking on the phone. He'd never been one to engage in long conversations on the phone and in fact disliked doing anything on it but exchanging vital information. "If I'm going to talk to someone, I need to see their eyes," he always said. But there is also the chance that he's having second thoughts about seeing me at all. Well, I've come too far to hear that on the phone; if he's changed his mind, let him tell me face-to-face.

All I say to the others, though, is "I'm wondering if we should wait until morning. We may get there too late. He might be asleep."

"I think we'll get to Cleveland in another couple of hours or so, maybe around nine," Joni says. "And then we'll have to find his house, but that shouldn't be so hard. So we'd probably be there by around nine or ten at the latest. You really think he'll be asleep then?"

"He might be. I'll be tired. I'm tired now. I think maybe we should wait until morning. Let's just stop for the night and go in the morning. I want to take a shower and look . . . you know."

"Well, you should call and tell him, then," Lise says. "In fact, I don't know why you didn't call him a long time ago and let him know we'd be late."

"My phone is dead," I say, which is true. Then, before anyone can volunteer the use of their phone, I say, "And anyway, I think it would be fun to surprise him. God knows he did plenty of that with me." What I don't add is that I, too, am phone-averse. Penny used to say I wasn't a real woman, the way I didn't go in for long conversations while holding a receiver to my ear. Even when I was a teenager, someone would start a good story, and I'd say, "Can you just come over?" I'd always thought that if Dennis and I ever did become a long-term couple, that would be one of the things that made us odd to others but deeply comfortable with each other.

"But what if he's not even there when we get there?" Lise asks.

"All right; I'll call him in the morning," I say, a little more emphatically than I need to.

"Okay, so . . . motel?" Renie asks.

"How about bowling, first?" Joni says. "It's too early to go to a motel." There's a place coming up on the right, Super Bowl, featuring a big neon sign of flying pins.

"I don't want to go bowling," Lise says, and Renie says, "I do." They wait for my vote; we have been honoring the democratic process.

"I'm in," I say. "I could use a beer and some humiliation." I am a terrible bowler, unless you change the rules and count a gutter ball as a strike. Which I am going to suggest.

"I thought you were tired!" Lise says.

"Not for bowling."

"You are *ner*vous."

"Maybe," I say.

I am, of course, but it's more than that. *What's the worst that could happen?* I've asked myself, many times over. But as we get closer, what worries me is what could not happen, how we could both be standing with popped balloons in our hands, planning our exit strategy fifteen minutes after we've said hello. Or the other possibility: that one will be disappointed, the other starry-eyed.

The idea of all of this has been so thrilling. But what can happen that will live up to the anticipation? How can we keep from being dismayed by the ways in which we've changed? He has told me how he looks, and I know he knows I'm no longer the black-haired girl he once knew. Still, I suspect that in each of our brains, in each of our minds' eyes, is firmly fixed an image from so long ago that it will be hard to reconcile the differences. Even someone who drives past a house she used to live in and finds it changed feels it in the gut.

A couple of years ago, I came across a set of photos a girlfriend had taken of me to give to the guy du jour. This was a very handsome guy aptly named Ken, if you consider the plastic perfection of Barbie's boyfriend of the same name. My Ken was going to law school and in possession of some impressive musical talent. He could play guitar like Leo Kottke, he could play piano and the ukulele, and he wrote songs. Unfortunately, that was about it. He was not good in conversation; he had no sense of irony or playfulness; he favored minute planning over spontaneity; he was, as my friend Donna put it, how gray got born. When I defended him to her, she said, "Oh, you just can't admit you fell for a piece of ass."

It was true, as it happened, but until I was willing to admit that to myself, I was trying to win him. To that end, Donna took some flattering pictures of me. I thought it was really generous of her, given her opinion of the intended recipient. I gave him the photos, about which he said, "Nice," and then he tossed them into a drawer with his condoms, which were red, which always used to make me kind of upset.

Last year, I found the negatives for those photos and had prints made, and when I picked them up, the images shocked me. I had been along for the ride, getting older, the changes had come gradually, but when I saw those pictures of me then versus me now, it was devastating. I thought of all I had lost and all that I had yet to lose, I thought of how youth is wasted on the young, and then I came to my senses and sent a donation to Doctors Without Borders and took a walk. But. Dennis will have a photo experience, so to speak, and so will I. And although how we look doesn't matter nearly so much as what we are, what we are is old enough that there are probably not all that many good years left. So what's the point?

"Nurse or purse, that's all a guy would want us for now," I overheard a woman about my age telling another. I suppose she might be right. And yet some stubborn part of me thinks otherwise. Don't we all want company in some form, are we not attracted to the idea of a body beside us in a thunderstorm, or another voice to help decide on dinner, to share astonishment at the latest political buffoonery or appreciation for the lush sets on *Downton Abbey*? Are we not, at our most basic, social animals, people who need other people, whether we want to or not?

But I have that now, in the company of these women I live with. It's true that we don't give each other the intimacy of a romantic love, and I guess if I'm honest I have to admit I'm not past wanting that. I guess I want to be like the old couples I sometimes see whose love still burns so bright it makes me stop and stare.

I watch the bowling balls rolling down the alley and the pins flying up in the air and think about how one of the hardest things in life is fessing up to what you want most, because if you do that, and you don't get it, it's so hard to be without it. I wonder if most people fully invest in what they care about most. There is a Kazantzakis quote I once taped to my computer that said, *I hope for nothing. I fear nothing. I am free.* But I took it off because the truth is that although I might have admired the words and anyone who might be able to honestly say them, they were very far away from the person I am. I live in fear of a lot of things. I recognize that I am not free. And all my life, I have hoped for everything.

A face comes up into my line of vision like a rising moon. Renie. "Helllllooooo," she says, and I laugh, and she says, "Your turn," and then, "What were you *thinking* about?"

"Nothing."

"Liar," she says.

"Liar," I agree. I grab a ball, squint at my adversaries all lined up at the end of my lane, and think about how I might actually knock some of them down. Then I let go of the ball, which bounces (as much as a bowling ball can) before it rolls leisurely toward the end of the lane. Regrettably, it is not my lane. I knock three pins down in the next lane over, and the guy who's bowling there is pissed.

"What the fuck!" he says, slamming down his ball. He comes over to me, his hands on his hips. I see a lot of coarse black hair curling out of the V at the top of his shirt and I just don't know what to do.

"I'm sorry, I'm sorry," I say. He is wearing a black bowling shirt and lots of gold jewelry that is lacking only a Playboy logo or some other demeaning image of women like that so often displayed on the mud flaps of eighteen-wheelers.

"You think this is funny?" the man asks. Oh God, he's at least six three.

"No, I think this is scary. And I'm sorry. I'm just a really bad bowler."

He nods in a kind of calculating way, the way a lot of men look when they're tonguing a toothpick, but then seems unable to think of anything else to say. He goes back over to his lane and picks up his ball. On the bench, a thin, curly-headed blonde sits staring at the floor. "Get me a beer, goddamnit," he yells at her, and the woman jumps up.

"Get it yourself, you pig!" Renie yells at him.

He starts toward her, and I say, "Relax, we're going, see? We're leaving." I pull on Renie's hand. Joni and Lise have already fled.

I walk out quickly, my heart racing, holding back laughter. I'm wide awake, thrilled. There's nothing like getting in trouble to make you feel young.

IN THE MORNING, I AM MUCH MORE AT EASE ABOUT SEEING DENNIS. I am, in fact, full of optimism. In a worst-case scenario, it will be interesting to see him again, and I know I'll at least like him. I call his cellphone to tell him we're going to get breakfast and then we'll be on our way, but he doesn't answer. I get one of those recorded voices that asks you to leave a message, which always makes me wonder if I'm really talking to the person I intend to. Nonetheless, I make my voice cheerful and confident and say, "Hi! I'm sorry we never made it over last night; we got in really late and I didn't want to wake you. But we're close now, we should be there by ten! So I guess we'll go and get some breakfast and then I'll call you back. You must be . . . Well, I don't know where you must be, but I'll call you back. Or call me, I think you have the number, or it will show up on your phone, of course. I'll see you soon."

Renie stretches and says, "I want some pancakes, does anyone else want pancakes?"

"I want something lighter," Joni says. "Enough already with all this ballast."

"All right, we'll ask at the desk for a hippie café," Renie says. "Maybe there's one on the way to Dennis's house." She looks over at me and I look away.

———

WE FIND A PLACE called Aunt Bea's with hive-shaped jars of honey
on wooden tables and lots of local artwork on the walls. There is a
corner of the restaurant with big fat old-fashioned upholstered chairs
given over to the computer users so they don't hog the tables. I point
to that area and say, "See? Good idea. Last time I went to Panera, I
couldn't find a table. I was walking around and around with my tray,
and all these people were sitting at the tables with their computers.
One woman hadn't even bought anything; she just had one of those
plastic cups with water. I kept walking past her but she wouldn't
move any of her papers spread all over the table."

"You know what you do in a situation like that?" Renie says.

I sigh. "Of course. Go over to the person and say, 'Would you mind
moving your papers so I can sit down?'"

"Exactement."

"Oh, that's so tiresome," Lise says. "It's like bad behavior in movie
theaters. People act like they're in their living rooms. That's why I
bought such a big TV screen, so I could act like my living room was a
movie theater."

Joni squirts honey in her herbal tea. "Plus who wants to sit with a
table hogger who obviously doesn't want to share? They'd be giving
you dirty looks even if they weren't looking at you."

Lise's phone rings and she looks at the number and doesn't answer.

"Sandy?" I ask, and she shakes her head no.

"Was it *him*?" Joni asks.

"Who?"

Joni frowns at her.

"*Yes,*" Lise says. "And I'll call him back later."

"Uh-oh," Renie says

"Never mind, you don't know," Lise says.

"Yes, I do," Renie says. "I knew you wouldn't let this happen. You're too scared. You want to be in control all the time."

I expect an argument, but Lise says nothing, sits staring at her plate. Finally, she says, "Maybe you're right. I'm used to being in control. I always was the fix-it person. Birds with broken wings, abandoned baby rabbits. I used to try to rebuild anthills that got knocked over. The thing I wanted most for Christmas every year was a *real* first aid kit. My parents kept giving me kid ones, but I wanted suture sets, IV equipment, I wanted a cut-down tray in case I had to do an emergency tracheotomy. My Uncle Will was a doctor and he used to let me come to work with him sometimes when he moonlighted in this little hospital's ER; I knew a stack of Band-Aids, pink candy pills, and a plastic stethoscope weren't good for anything." She looks up at Renie. "But to your point. Honestly? I am scared. I don't know if I can take the chance that in trying to work together again, we'll crash on the rocks again. Even if I keep Sandy out of it, at least at first, I don't know if it's good for me. I feel like I've been acting so foolishly."

"Maybe it's good for you to act a little foolish," Joni says. "You've been . . . I don't know, more fun on this road trip than I've ever seen you be."

"Why don't you just relax and take it one step at a time?" Renie says.

"We're on Cece now," Lise says, flinging her napkin onto her plate. She looks over at me. "Call Dennis and tell him we're on the way."

I dial the number and get the same message. "Huh. Still no answer."

"Do you think he's sleeping?" Joni asks.

"I don't know." It's eight o'clock, one of those could-go-either-way hours.

"He might have gotten up a lot last night," Lise says.

Almost reflexively, it occurs to me to say, "No he didn't," but how do I know?

"Let's just go over there," Renie says. "Cece can call him from the car when we're sitting outside his house. *That'll* be a surprise! Give me the keys, Lise; I'll drive. I want to go through a McDonald's drive-through on the way over and get a real breakfast."

"You just had a real breakfast," Lise says, and Renie says, "Granola with all that self-righteous fruit and nuts is not a breakfast. It is a punishment. It is a prescription. It is mortar for building—"

"All right," Lise says. "Let's go."

"Be right there," I say. "I have to pee."

I don't have to pee, but I pee anyway. Then I brush my teeth and my gums and my tongue and the roof of my mouth and under my tongue. I put on a shade of lipstick that is very subtle, that just makes you appear to have circulating blood. I rat up my hair a little on top and on the sides; it's so much thinner than before. I adjust my brassiere; last time I saw him, I never wore one. Oh, those wonderful days of free breasts, but I'm glad I came back to Brylcreem, so to speak.

Not long ago, I saw an interview with a fiery feminist of yore, someone not quite Gloria Steinem but close, a woman who in her prime stood before thousands of cheering young women who were coming into a kind of power they'd never known before. And all respect, truly, but apparently this woman had never come back to bras, and the look was . . . Well, you would have to be a less superficial person than I not to fixate on all that lowness.

I stand back from the mirror, look at my worried face, then hike up my purse on my shoulder, smile, and go forth to complete my mission. It comes to me that there is no place on earth I would rather be. If someone came up to me and said, "Surprise, you've just won tickets to go anywhere you want right now, all expenses paid," I'd say, "That's okay. I'm going to see Dennis Halsinger."

I get into the front seat beside Renie, who has put the address into the GPS. According to it, we are 107.3 miles away. Then, after we leave the parking lot, 107.2.

It takes us a bit under two hours to get to the city limits. When we finally get to Dennis's quiet street, it's hard to see the numbers on the houses. The GPS has told us we have *arrived* at our destin*ation*, but we can't quite make out exactly where that destination is. Finally Lise points to a small green house set back from the curb and says, "There it is!"

"Okay," I say. "Okay, here goes." I dial Dennis's number again, and get the same recording. I snap my phone shut. "Let's go; I think he changed his mind."

"He didn't change his mind," Joni says. "Go and ring the doorbell. We'll wait here."

I get out of the car and sneak a look at the upstairs, then downstairs windows to see if he is peeking out, but I don't see anything. When I get to the door, I see that there's an envelope tucked in the screen door with my name on it. There's something hard inside, a key, I think. I open the envelope and yes, that's exactly what it is, along with a note to me:

Cece,

   Don't know what happened; you never did call last night. I tried calling you a bunch of times yesterday and got no answer, hope you're okay. Depending on when you get this, I'm either on a plane to or in Paris. A good friend of mine is the editor of the travel section of the paper here, and he called yesterday to ask if I'd fill in for a shoot they're doing in Montmartre—the guy they were going to send all of a sudden got sick, and I need the work.

I'm only going to be there for a few days or so, and I'll call you when I'm back. Doubt there'll be much time for fun there; if this shoot is like the others I've been on, I'll work eighteen hours, get back to the hotel, and fall flat on my face.

Anyway, here's the key if you need a place to stay; they're not coming to empty it out for ten days. Check out my mom's decor; it'll break your heart. Help yourself to any food.

> *Don't know why*
> *you never called.*
> *Dennis*

I read the note once more, then turn around to wave the others in.

WHAT DOES A HOUSE'S CONTENTS SAY ABOUT A PERSON? A lot, I think. I hardly have to cross the threshold before I get an idea of what Dennis's mother was like. I think she, like many of the women of her generation, was inordinately neat and clean. I think she bought some good furniture when she married, and stuck with it: the wood is maple, and the style is colonial. In the kitchen there's a cream pitcher hanging by a hook above the table, as well as a framed sampler saying NO MATTER WHERE I SERVE MY GUESTS/IT SEEMS THEY LIKE MY KITCHEN BEST. There's a row of chimera African violets along the windowsill over the sink; apparently Dennis has been keeping them alive.

In the living room, there are crisscross sheers across the front window; a tall grandfather clock, gone silent now; a bowl of butterscotch candy on an end table, next to the La-Z-Boy chair that offers the best view of the television. In the dining room, there's a braided rug, a framed print of Norman Rockwell's family at Thanksgiving, and a cup rack featuring matching cups and saucers as well as a spoon rack with tiny spoons from everywhere. There's a crocheted tablecloth and a hutch that holds the good china, some pieces on display.

"My Aunt Tootie had a house like this," Joni says, when I rejoin her in the kitchen. Her voice is low, as though we're in a funeral parlor, and in some respects I suppose we are. "She had a cleaning cart and I think it was her favorite thing in the world. It was where she kept everything she needed, including newspaper and vinegar for the windows, and ammonia for the oven. She loved cleaning." She moves over to the pantry. "I'll bet there are cans with expiration dates from years ago in here." She picks up a can of tomatoes, turns it upside down. "Yup."

"Don't be so judgmental about a woman who just died," Renie says. "And stop snooping."

"We can look," I say. "Dennis told us to look. I'm going upstairs."

The first room I come to is his mother's bedroom, a study in blue: the walls, the curtains, the quilted bedspread. There's a long dresser with a perfume tray and framed photos. One is of Dennis, his high school graduation picture, I think. He was a handsome boy with a Beatle cut, and an I'm-so-getting-out-of-here look in his eyes. There are two framed photos on the wall that I think Dennis might have taken. One is a candid of his parents at the edge of the Grand Canyon: his father is pointing, his mother has her hand over her mouth. The other is of a group of boys at an A&W gathered around the open hood of a '57 Bel Air, staring mesmerized at the engine while behind them a pretty spectacularly endowed waitress on roller skates holds a tray of burgers and mugs of root beer high in the air and is ignored.

There is a powder-blue velvet armchair in the corner of the room, a scrapbook propped up against it. In it are photos of Dennis's parents in their youth, then many of Dennis as a baby, riding his rocking horse, sitting in a high chair with birthday cake plastered all over his face, triumphantly atop his father's shoulders. At the back are love letters, I think, sent to his mother in 1943; letters from the front, judging from the APO return address of SFC Carl Halsinger. They're bound in blue ribbon, the ribbon so old it's fragile now. I know Dennis's parents are both dead, but I don't open even one.

There's a separate envelope, no stamp, and a single line as an address: *To Dennis's future wife.*

I swallow, then untuck the flap to see what's inside. There are several pages of recipes, and the note on top says:

Hello there,

If you are reading this, I am glad of it, wherever I am. I always thought I'd dance at my son's wedding, but life has its own agenda. I'm awfully sorry not to meet you and to tell you in person what a wonderful man you're getting, but then I guess you know that. Here are a bunch of recipes for Dennis's favorite foods that I used to make for him. It's a tradition in our family that the new wife gets some old recipes and I'm very glad to pass these on.

It is also our tradition to pass on some words of wisdom about how to have a happy marriage. I know a lot of people say things about don't go to bed angry, start and end each day with a kiss, be together but also spend some time apart, that sort of thing. For me, I guess it can all be summed up this way: Pay attention. The rest falls into place with that, I think.

I hope you live in happiness for a very long time. My husband and I sure did.

> *Very best wishes,*
> *Janet Halsinger*

I page through some of the recipes: Italian spaghetti, Captain's Chicken, Pudding in a Poke, Cheesiest Macaroni and Cheese, Lemon Icebox Cake, Tricolor Macaroni Salad.

I put the recipes and the letter back into the envelope. The blue ribbon holding the pack of letters from her husband has slid to the end and I move it carefully to the middle, then tuck the letters back into the scrapbook. I put the scrapbook back beside the chair.

I wonder if Dennis's mother sat here and looked at this album, her mind released from whatever failings she was experiencing and returned to her days of being a young mother in a print housedress and red lipstick, pulling the shades and putting her baby down for a nap, then going down into the kitchen to pore over her *Settlement Cook Book* for new ideas. Or returned to an even earlier time, when she was a young woman whose man was overseas, and she lay on her bed each night with her eyes closed tightly, her rosary in her hands. So strange: you uncap the pen and put down some thoughts in your head, some feelings in your heart, never thinking about what they will become so many years later, not understanding that you're making such a treasure out of ink and pulp. I wonder how recently she wrote the letter to put in with the recipes.

The next bedroom, the one overlooking the backyard, is Dennis's. There are a couple of shirts and a pair of jeans on the bed, probably what he chose not to pack or couldn't fit in his suitcase. I pick up the jeans and look at the waistline; he hasn't gained any more weight than I have. There is a tripod in the corner, and a large black bag that I assume holds more equipment. I pick up one of the shirts and smell it: only detergent. I sit on the edge of the bed, and then lie down cautiously, as though there's another person there whom I don't want to awaken. I close my eyes and a kind of comfort comes to me, like a cat curled up on my belly. I miss him suddenly, this man I've not seen in so many years, miss him deeply and sorrowfully. He feels, suddenly, so known to me. The pictures I saw of him here, I suppose. I knew a woman whose marriage was in big trouble, and when they went to a counselor she suggested they each look at photos of the other as children.

I move to the windowsill Dennis told me he used to watch his parents from and stand there with my arms crossed, looking out into the yard where azaleas and hydrangeas and Stargazer lilies bloom. I wonder how old Dennis's parents were when they moved here; if they stood in the backyard shading their eyes against the sun to look up at these windows and thought, *This is our house, we'll never leave it.*

By the time I get back downstairs, Renie has gone to the car and come back with her computer. She goes into the living room and stretches out on the sofa. "I'm going to work for a while. I need to address someone who's fifty years old and suffering the junior high–level abuse of a co-worker who used to be her friend. The rest of you can dishonor a dead person."

"It feels more like honoring, to me," I say. I start to tell her about the photo album, but then don't: I want to keep it to myself.

"There's cold cuts and rolls and potato salad and beer in the fridge," she says. "Thank God. Oh, and there's a bag of Oreos in the pantry with a big ribbon on them."

"Because they used to be my favorite," I say. "I used to offer him some every time he came over."

Joni and Lise come up from the basement. "She canned," Joni says. "It's unbelievable what's down there. Asparagus and beets and green beans and corn and cherries and peaches and pears. And sauerkraut. And pickles. And peppers. All those jars, all lined up. God, they're beautiful."

She moves to the little kitchen table and sits down, looks around. Then she slams her hand on the table. "That's it. I've made the decision. I'm ready."

"Ready for what?" I say.

"I want to give people what was offered here. Comfort food. In

warm surroundings, none of that pretense. I want to open a restaurant and serve food inspired by what I'll bet was cooked here. I want
my own restaurant, and I'll have the kinds of things I make for you
guys, at home."

I think about the recipes I just saw. When I see Dennis, I'll ask if
Joni can have copies.

"Oh, I can't believe it, I'm so excited! I'm going to do it! I have
money saved and I'll take out a business loan and I'll find a good location and I'll do it!

"And it will be so much fun. I want it to be like it's in the fifties and
you're going over to a house like this one and my Aunt Tootie's, where
you'll sit down and eat meat loaf and mashed potatoes and apple pie
only it will be turkey meat loaf and lighter mashed potatoes and apple
pie. All those bib aprons I've found at the Goodwill? I'm going to
cook in them. And all those embroidered tablecloths I've collected—
I'll put one on every table. I'll have mason jars of fresh flowers on
every table, too. All the dishes will be different, all the silverware. I'm
going to put a television in front so if you have to wait for a table you
can watch reruns of old shows like *Father Knows Best* and *Leave It to
Beaver*."

"Call it Aunt Tootie's," Renie says.

Joni looks at her. "Nope. I'm calling it the Tomato Soup and
Toasted Cheese Café."

Renie shrugs. "I'd go there."

"You want some quilts to put on the wall?" I ask.

"Yes! And the sign will have two round faces, a boy with a cap
turned sideways and a girl with a big bow in her hair, and they'll be
licking their chops."

"Want a part-time waitress who'll work for food?" I ask.

She looks at me, grinning. "Really?"

"Really."

She grabs her purse. "Let's go. I'm going to find things for the restaurant in every town we go through, from now on. I wish I'd gotten every funky salt and pepper shaker we saw."

"Oh, there'll be more of those," Lise says. She looks at her watch. "Should we get going?"

"Let me just check my email to see if they had any problems with the column I sent yesterday," Renie says. She brings it up and says, "Oh wow, my daughter."

She looks up at the rest of us. "I'm not sharing." She reads it, nods. "It's good."

BEFORE WE GET BACK in the car, I volunteer to take Riley for a walk in one direction while the others go the opposite way. They want to speed-walk, and Riley's pace is more . . . contemplative. When you're in a hurry, it can get on your nerves. When you're not, it's enjoyable.

I am almost back to the house when my cellphone rings. When I answer, there is a long pause, and then I hear, "Cece?"

"*Dennis?*"

We both start laughing and then together say, "How are you?"

"I'm glad you're alive!" he says.

"I'm sorry I didn't call."

"Hold on," he says, "can you hold on?"

"Sure!"

I stand still, waiting for him to come back to the phone. I'm so excited. His voice sounds exactly the same to me. Dennis Halsinger.

"Cece?"

"Yeah!"

"I'm sorry; I guess I shouldn't have tried to call. I have to go. They don't give me one second, this shoot is murder. I'll call you when I'm back in the States. *Answer* that time!"

"I will," I say. "And Dennis?"

Nothing. He's gone.

I put my phone back in my pocket, and it rings again. Good. Now I can see if he can give me a time frame.

But the number that shows up is the Arms, and I answer saying, "Michael?"

"It's Annie," she says. "Are you able to talk for a minute?"

I stop walking, then, dry-mouthed, say, "Yes." *Don't say he died.*

"I'm calling to let you know that Michael and Phoebe are getting married tomorrow."

"*What?*" I say, laughing. This information collides so hard with what I feared that at first I can't process it.

I can hear the smile in Annie's voice when she says, "It turns out that Phoebe is pregnant. That's why she was so insistent about seeing him; she wanted to tell him, and to give him the option of giving the baby his name. He really wanted you to come, and in fact he was going to wait until you returned and ask you to come for a visit, then surprise you with the ceremony. But he's . . . Well, he's decided to go ahead and do it tomorrow. He didn't want to tell you, he didn't want to interrupt your vacation. But I thought I would let you know in case you wanted to come."

"What time will it be?"

"Six o'clock tomorrow evening. That's as soon as the minister Phoebe likes can get here."

"I've got frequent-flier miles; I'll come home as soon as I can."

"Good. Shall I tell him?"

"I don't know; what do you think? I'd kind of like to surprise him."

"Do that, then," Annie says. "And I'm so glad you're coming. He credits you for his getting back with her, you know."

"He would have, anyway."

"Perhaps. It will be good to see you, Cece. I'm so glad you're coming."

"Me, too."

I snap the phone shut and stand still on the sidewalk for a while. There are instances when everything around you grows suddenly more vibrant and precious, and this is one of them. I am so happy for the postcard Dennis sent me: look at all it has brought me. I'm so much more alive than I've been; I'm so much happier. I realize I am looking forward to things in a way I feared I never would again.

"Let's go," I tell Riley and head back to the house. I've loved being on this trip, but now I want to go home and go to a wedding.

AT THE AIRPORT, after I get through security, I arrive at the gate fifteen minutes before it's time to board. I sit next to a young mother whose little girl, maybe three years old, would apparently rather be anywhere but here.

After the little girl emits a shriek that comes close to shattering the plate-glass window behind us, the woman apologizes.

"It's okay," I say, but naturally I'm thinking, *Oh, please don't let me have a seat anywhere near hers.*

"I'm going to let her run for a few minutes," the woman says. "Don't let the plane leave without us."

"Okay," I say, as if I can really do anything much about that, and watch the woman carry the little girl out to the walkway. She puts her down, says, "Here I come!" and the girl stops crying and takes off running.

After a few minutes there is the call for boarding and I look to see if I can find the mother, but she is nowhere in sight. I tell the gate agent who scans my boarding pass that a young mother and a little girl have taken off down the walkway, and they are on this flight. She shrugs.

"So . . ." I say.

"Pardon me, please." She reaches around me for the next passenger's boarding pass. I look behind me once more, then move toward the jetway.

Once inside the plane, I settle myself into the window seat. The two seats next to me are empty, and I'm pretty sure I know who will sit there.

Right. I hear a familiar screeching, and here comes the mother rushing after the daughter, saying, "Lindsey, come back here!" She grabs her daughter by the arm and half drags her to my row.

"Oh, *hi!*" the mother says.

I try to respond equally enthusiatically.

Lindsey gets put in the middle seat. And apparently she would prefer that her seat belt not be put on her. The decibel level rises and people all around are muttering and scowling. "Want me to try?" I ask, and the poor mother nods.

"Hey, Lindsey," I say, and she stops screaming long enough to regard me suspiciously.

"Did you know this belt is magical?"

No response, but at least the screaming has stopped.

I lean in closer. "If I put it on you, this airplane will lift right up into the air and *you* will get a surprise. But you have to sit down and let me put it around you." *Surprise,* I'm thinking, *what can the surprise be?* I decide I'll give her the SkyMall catalogue and tell her to find something she really really wants and who knows, she might just get it.

She sits down, and I snap the seat belt around her. Then I say, "Tell your mommy to wipe your nose, okay?"

She does. Then the plane starts to taxi and I close my eyes and wonder what Joni and Lise and Renie are doing. For the first time since I made the decision to come off the road, I regret it. I think about Lise and the glittery star-shaped sunglasses she found in a travel mart a couple of days ago and has worn since she bought them. I think about the sign we saw advertising PUPPIES FOR SALE, and how we had such a good time playing on the lawn with a litter of seven-week-old goldens. "I have to tell you we're not going to buy one," I told the woman who owned the dogs, and she said, "That's all right, they need the socialization."

I think of the time we watched a local production of *A Midsummer Night's Dream* that was performed outdoors, of the garden party that Renie said she was sure we could wander into unnoticed, but we were noticed, all right. And asked very nicely to leave.

I feel a tapping on my arm. "Where is my surprise?" Lindsey whispers.

I look over at her mother, who appears to be asleep.

"It's coming," I whisper back, thinking that if I give her the Sky-Mall catalogue now, a howling protest may follow. "In the meantime, how about we just have a little conversation?"

"'Bout what?"

About what? Good question. I lean in closer to her. "Do you think everyone is carrying a heavy burden?"

"No. I'm not. And needer are you."

I stare into her face. I try to imagine what she'll look like when she gets older. "Do you have crayons in your backpack?"

"No. I have glitter markers. And I have coloring books and only one doll who is Cassandra and M&M's and Go Fish." She sighs then, a deep and dramatic sigh, as if someone has asked her to relieve Sisyphus.

"Well," I say. "Would you like to color?"

She nods, and digs in her backpack for markers and her coloring books. "Do you want farm animals or fairy princesses?" she asks.

"Farm animals," I say, and she says, "Good, because I want the fairy princesses because the farm animals are boring."

"Okay, let me ask you this: Do any of your fairy princesses have four chambers in their stomachs?"

"What is *chambers*?"

"It's like little rooms."

"Nothing has little rooms in its stomach."

"Cows do."

She looks over at my coloring book, at the cow page I'm on. Then she continues coloring the jewels in her fairy's crown, which, I have to admit, looks like much more fun to color than this cow, which is looking out from the page like it's my responsibility to think of everything. A lock of Lindsey's hair is hanging in her eyes, and I reach out to gently tuck it behind her ear. This makes for a familiar pain in my four-chambered heart, acknowledgment that I will never have a child to raise, or grandchildren to spoil. I look out the window for a moment, then ask Lindsey if she has a black marker.

After she gives it to me, I start to color my cow, making it a Holstein, and then I ask Lindsey if she has a gold marker. When she gives me that, I draw my cow a crown. Lindsey watches with interest. "It is still not a princess," she says.

————

AFTER I GET HOME from the airport, I carry my suitcase up to my room, open the windows, and then go back outside. There's a good hour of light left, and I head over toward Como Park. I'll walk around the lake on the pedestrian path. Penny and I took this walk sometimes, and I remember once she talked about how grateful she was for the effort that went into making the place so user-friendly, so beautiful to behold. I see wildflowers that look like little white stars in the grass. Willow trees dip their branches into the water as though stirring up the minnows. I watch the gossipy red-winged blackbirds gather for the night in the high branches of a tree, and the cranes standing motionless in the reeds. The water has smoothed out, as if it has been tucked in for the night, and the sky turns a smudged charcoal pink at the horizon. I pick up my pace so that I can get home before dark. I walk with my head down, my hands in my pockets. All these firsts, these times of doing things without her that I used to do with her, are getting easier.

When I get back to the house, it's dark enough that I have to find the keyhole by touch. I let myself in, turn on a few lights downstairs, and put water on to boil for some pasta. I'd intended to go out for dinner—there's not much in the refrigerator—but now I find that I want to stay here. And besides, I always love an excuse for eating noodles and butter and Parmesan cheese. I hope Joni will have that at her restaurant.

THE NEXT AFTERNOON, I FIND A STACK OF MAIL ON THE WELCOME mat. Our neighbor had been keeping it for us; she must have seen that I'm home. It's the usual assortment of junk mail, junk mail designed not to look like junk mail, and bills. But then I spy a postcard, addressed to me, a picture of a Métro stop in Paris. On the back, these lines in his customary black ink:

Well, croissants and cobblestones and lace curtains and
breathtaking beauty almost everywhere you turn. I've been
assigned a couple more things to shoot, shouldn't take more than
a day or two if the weather holds. And then you know what
comes next. More or less.
    À bientôt.

I put the postcard in my purse and head over to the Arms. I'm really looking forward to seeing Michael again.

Annie is with someone when I arrive, and I wait for her for a while, then decide to go up to Michael's room. The door is closed, and I knock softly. It is opened by Phoebe, and what I see in the room behind her takes my breath away. There are long pieces of sheer white fabric tacked up on the walls, which makes for a softening effect, an ethereal effect, and there are candles everywhere. It's a cliché by now, an overabundance of candles, but here it just seems right. They are white candles, all the same size, and they are all lit already, though the ceremony is twenty-five minutes away. Phoebe puts her finger to her lips: I can see that, behind her, Michael is sleeping. She points to the hallway and I follow her out there.

"I'm so glad you came," she says. In the light of the hallway, I can see better the simple but very pretty long dress she is wearing, white lace, sleeveless; and she has flowers in her hair. My eyes fill with tears and she takes my arm and says, "Don't cry, or I will," and I get hold of myself immediately.

"How are you?" Phoebe says, and I say, "How are *you*?"

She takes a big breath in, shakes her head, and smiles. "There's so much."

I say nothing, wait.

"I . . . Did you hear that I'm pregnant?"

"Yes, Annie told me. I hope that was okay."

"It's fine. I love that I'm pregnant. I'm so happy I'm pregnant. It's something Michael and I had agreed upon, that we'd use artificial insemination; he donated sperm before he started his treatment, we did all the paperwork and signed all the forms so we'd be all set whenever we decided the time was right. And I went for the appointment we'd made two days after we came apart. I couldn't reach Michael to see if it was still okay with him; he wouldn't talk to me. So I just did it on my own. I figured I'd give it one try, and if it worked, it was meant to be."

"How is he?" I ask.

She looks over at me. "Maybe a week. When he's awake, we talk. It means everything. When I kept trying to see him, it was because I wanted him to know about the baby, yes, but mostly I just wanted to talk to him. Talking to Michael has always felt to me like . . . like being held. I knew as soon as I met him that he was the one for me. I knew it right away. And so did he. We moved in together two weeks after we met. Everyone said we shouldn't, but I'm so glad we did."

She looks at her watch. "It's almost time. Would you go and see if the minister is there? I just want a minute alone." ·

"Of course." I go into Michael's room and find both the minister and Annie with him. Michael looks like he has just woken up.

"Hey," he says, smiling. "You want to be my best man?"

"Absolutely."

I stand by Michael's side and I watch his face as Phoebe comes in, watch him as the minister says the few brief things he has to say: *True love's fullness is not bound or measured by time; we are here to bear witness to an occasion of joy*, et cetera, et cetera. I watch Michael slide a thin gold band onto Phoebe's finger and watch her slide a matching band onto his. It's too big for him, I can tell, but it will stay on. I stand back as Phoebe gently kisses his mouth, then his cheek, then his forehead, then his mouth again, weeping, smiling, and then I look away because I can't look anymore, it's like staring into the sun.

IN THE MORNING, THE MAIL ARRIVES EARLY. I REACH INTO THE box and find another postcard from Dennis. This one, still postmarked Paris but with no date, says:

Late flight out of Paris in a few days. Can't quite imagine what it will be like to see you again. Not for lack of trying.

I read the message again. Flight to where? Cleveland? Minneapolis? When the phone rings, I answer excitedly. It couldn't be him yet, could it?

"What are you doing?" Joni asks.

So it's not him saying, "I'm at the airport; come and get me."

"Making breakfast."

"We just had breakfast—at a spa! It was such a beautiful breakfast I photographed it. Lemon ricotta pancakes, very light, with blackberries and strawberries and boysenberry syrup and edible flowers, too."

"Lovely."

"We miss you. Fly out here, and we'll drive back together."

"No, I . . . I'm going to stay here now. I got a postcard from Dennis. I think he's coming here."

"When?!"

"I don't know. He sent a postcard but didn't specify dates. So how's Renie doing at a spa? She told me she hates spas."

She laughs. "Not anymore! She got a hot stone massage yesterday. I think she has a crush on Loni, one of the masseuses. Well, we all do. Later today, we're going to the Pool of Rising Consciousness, and then we're going to get a seaweed wrap, and tonight it's candlelight yoga."

"Oh? Well, I'll be cleaning the house later, so you're not the only one who knows how to have fun."

"How was the wedding, Cece?"

"It was beautiful."

She waits, but I don't want to say more.

"Listen," she says. "We're going to stay another day here and then start back. So look for us in . . . maybe three or four days? If Dennis comes, hang a flag outside if we need not to come in."

"Very funny."

"I'm serious. Oh, and guess what. Lise called Steve and he might be coming to see her soon. They've been talking and talking. Okay, I have to go. We miss you, we love you, we'll see you soon!"

THE NEXT MORNING, I put on a Bob Wills and His Texas Playboys CD, change into an old black T-shirt and jeans, put a bandanna over my hair, and go out into the garden. The crew I hired to help me did a fabulous job: I love the blue delphinium next to the sea of lavender. Wildflowers surround the flattened boulder I thought would be good for sitting on to meditate, or just sitting on, period. I work the soil a little, stake up some of the taller plants, do a little deadheading. It's a warm morning, in the eighties, and I can soon feel sunburn starting on my cheeks, across my nose.

It's beautiful out here. Just as good as your other garden.

"It will be. It needs more time."

I love the daisies.

"I put them in for you."

I know.

"*Do* you know?"

Nothing.

"Penny?"

I work for another hour or so, then sit down on the top front porch step to think about whether I might want to go to a movie tonight. I'm just about to go inside to see what's playing when a car pulls up to the curb. I watch as the man in the car sits still for a minute, then opens the door and gets out.

Dennis.

I yank the bandanna off my hair, fold my hands tightly together in my lap. As advertised, he's missing most of his hair. But there are those eyes.

I watch him come toward me and everything in me goes quiet. I feel like a stopped clock.

Just before he reaches me, I stand up.

But he sits down and stretches his long legs out before him. He's wearing a blue-and-white-striped dress shirt with the sleeves rolled halfway up his forearms, faded jeans, and black cowboy boots. He stares straight ahead to say, "I thought I'd shine my boots before I ask you to go dancing, but I'm going to have to ask you for the polish."

I sit down beside him and I can see the tension in his jaw. And at that moment, all my own fear goes away. I am his lover and his sister and his mother and his brother and his friend. I couldn't look worse and it couldn't matter less. All that matters is here we are. I say, "I've got polish. The rest, you don't have to ask for."

He smiles then.

We sit out there talking until there's a red sun hanging low in the sky. Then I take his hand and pull him up. There are eggs we can fry for supper. After that, I'll take a bath. And we'll see.

After he comes into the front hall with me, I say, "How about if we—"

"Yes," he says.

I COME INTO MY bedroom from my bath with a towel wrapped around me. Dennis is sitting at my desk, reading a book I keep on my nightstand, letters van Gogh wrote to his brother. "Listen to this," he says. And he reads me a quote: *"I have a terrible need of—shall I say the word?—religion. Then I go out and paint the stars."*

I nod, my throat tight, my heart full.

He turns off the overhead, and in the light of the moon, he takes his clothes off. And then he opens his arms and says, "This is how I was born."

I drop my towel.

He comes over to me and starts to lift me up—that same romantic, sweeping gesture—and drops me. We both fall to the floor, laughing.

"Are you okay?" he asks.

"I'm fine," I say, still laughing. "Are you?"

He puts my face between his hands and kisses me so sweetly I'm glad I've already fallen down.

Then he takes my hand and pulls me up and leads me to the bed. I'd thought, *Never again,* but I am so spectacularly wrong.

Two days later, I bring Dennis to my mother's for breakfast. I'd called and asked her if I might bring someone along for her to meet.

"Oh God, the hippie?" she asked.

"His name is Dennis, Mom. He's a photographer."

"Oh, my. He's back in town."

"I think you might like him if you give him half a chance."

"Well, do you think he could take a photo of me and Early Nelson?"

"Sure. What for?"

She doesn't answer.

"What for, Mom?"

"Now, we're just talking about it. But this way we won't have to pay someone on the day."

When we arrive and she opens the door, my mother gives Dennis a big smile, then a hug. "Well!" she says. "You turned out just fine!"

"Thank you," he says. "So did you."

She comes out into the hall with us, speaks quietly. "I want you two to meet Early. Don't say anything about our getting married, though. We agreed that we would give each other time to think. We've agreed on forty-eight hours."

"That's not much time," I say, laughing.

"We haven't *got* much time," she says, not laughing at all.

She turns to Dennis. "Honestly, though. Didn't you turn out just fine. You know, I have to tell you, I thought you'd still have that long hair."

"Wish I still did, I could paste some up on top," he says.

She opens the door wider, calls out "Early? Sweetheart?" and it doesn't bother me at all. She calls Early "sweetheart," and I imagine my father smiling.

DENNIS AND I have just come back from grocery shopping when the phone rings. I answer it expecting it to be my roommates; I'm going to share with them the news that Dennis has arrived. But it's not them; it's Annie. As soon as I hear her voice, I know.

"Was Phoebe with him?" I ask.

"Yes. It was very peaceful."

I swallow, start to cry, and I think, *I hate this. I hate this yin-yang life that is always pulling the rug out from beneath your feet.* I feel an odd rush of heat coming up my back and into my neck.

Dennis stops unpacking the grocery bags and comes to stand beside me.

He knows about Michael. He knows about how I want to continue to volunteer at the Arms. But now I tell him, "I'm not going there anymore. I've had enough. I'm not setting myself up for any more of this."

He says nothing, which I think means he's thinking the same thing I am: *Yes, you will.*

"It's so un*fair*!" I say, and what can he say to that? It's true.

Once, after one of my more bitter breakups, I sat slumped on my sofa with a pile of sodden Kleenex at my feet. It was three in the afternoon and I was still in my pajamas. Penny was trying to console me. "What's the point in loving anything when it will just change or be taken away?" I asked. And she said, "The point in loving is only that. And when you lose something, you have to remember that then there is room for the next thing. And there is always a next thing, Cece. I wish you would believe me."

LATE THAT NIGHT, I'm out sitting on the boulder in the garden. I'm thinking about a story I once heard about a woman who was told by a psychic that her death would be by water. The woman packed up and moved to the desert: no chance of drowning there! Instead, she ran out of water and died of thirst.

What good does it do to try to be master of your fate if it's the other way around?

And now I think of Penny, of the times since she died when I've felt so sure that she was near. It's not always hearing her voice, sometimes it's only a sense of something, as though she has just brushed by me or just left a room I've entered. How much of that is real and how much is just something you want so much you make yourself believe it's true? I don't know. If you asked my mother if those we've lost are still among us, she'd be as matter-of-factly sure of it as she is about the price of coffee. Once I said, "Well, if that's true, why doesn't everyone have the experience?"

"The dead don't come if they're not welcome," she said. "Not everyone wants to experience such a thing. Not everyone can handle it. Also they don't come if your reasons are suspect. And believe me, they know."

The morning after Dennis arrived, I was standing at the bathroom mirror and Penny came.

Good for you.

"Do you like him?" I asked my own image, and in my own eyes I saw her swirling around and around, her head back, something she called her happy dance. Then she stopped and leaned in very close to me, and I could see the gold flecks in her brown eyes, I could see them again.

Still. What good is it to believe in any kind of afterlife in the absence of hard evidence?

Oh, come on. Hard evidence is overrated.

I look up and smile, as though she might be standing there before me.

The best things in life have no hard evidence to support them. Hope. Faith. Love.

"I suppose that's true."

What are you doing out here all alone?

"I'm trying to figure things out. Help me."

I think you're doing fine on your own.

I hear the screen door bang shut and here comes Dennis, moving toward me in the darkness.

He says nothing, just sits next to me.

After a while, I say, "What do you make of death?"

He shrugs. "I think people see death as the hunter, but it's just the ticket taker, the timekeeper. It's the sound of a record playing in the background."

I nod. Then I say, "Maybe it's also there to remind us to do what we ought to."

"And what should you do, Cece?"

"Be here. Give more."

"What else?"

"I don't know. What do you think? What else should I do?"

"Be with me? Finally?"

I feel myself starting to cry and I put my hands over my face. He puts his arm around me and rocks me side to side, slowly, gently.

I think about the fortune Cosmina gave me, so long ago, which I have never forgotten: *Your task will be to learn in what direction to look for life's greatest riches.* I take my hands away from my face and look into his.

Fate is a part of our lives. Another part is choice. But the biggest part is the mystery, the great unknowable, about which we feel so many things, including joy.

I T'S BEEN A LITTLE OVER A YEAR SINCE I GOT THE POSTCARD
from Dennis that inspired the road trip. Dennis and I are living in a
coach house behind a big old house near Lake of the Isles, and it's full
only of the things we really love and use.

A lot of people worry about how a new relationship between older
people can work when those people are so set in their ways, as they
say. At least for now, I can report that it works beautifully: the only
fight we've had of any note occurred during a vacation we took right
after we moved in together, and like most spectacular fights, it was
about something stupid, I can't even remember what. We'd gone to
Rockport, Massachusetts, which is an artists' colony; I thought we'd
both like it there. And we did, we had a wonderful time, except for
the day we so bitterly argued. I think we were both just scared about
having moved in together, thinking, *What in the hell have I done?*

We went our separate ways that day. I walked for miles along the
ocean, and as the sun was beginning to set, I went back into town to
eat some dinner. I went into a small restaurant on Bearskin Neck with
a wooden sign proclaiming that the very best clam chowder in the
world was served there. When I walked in the door, I saw Dennis
sitting alone at a table, bent over his dinner. He didn't see me until I
was upon him, until I tapped his shoulder. When he looked up, I said
nothing. He gestured to the chair opposite him, and I sat down. "I'll

give you a bite, and you can decide for yourself," he said, holding out a spoonful of the chowder.

"I've already decided," I said, and he gave me one of his famous penetrating gazes and said, "Yeah. Me, too. I decided a long time ago."

This morning, in a chatty reverie, I told Penny about something Dennis said to me the other day. We were talking about photography and he said, "The greatest understanding of a thing is when you can't reduce it any further." For me, those words reverberated in so many directions at once.

We're hosting a potluck dinner tonight, Dennis and I. We're eating outside under the maple trees, at a long wooden table covered with a few of my sturdier quilts, set on point. When I first laid them out and stepped back to see how they looked, it was like seeing a row of people waiting for a show to start: sitting up straight, happily expectant, chatting quietly among themselves. I'd put out vases of peonies and roses, a candelabra. Now it's time to light the candles against the gathering dusk.

I go inside to the kitchen, for matches.

In the gloaming. We always liked that phrase.

"We always liked that time of day, the golden hour."

Yes, we liked how the colors changed, how they always seemed their richest selves, then.

I hear a burst of laughter and look out the window at the crowd of people, all so dear to me. There's Lise and Joni and Renie and their new roommate, Paula Martinez, a stained-glass artist. Phoebe and baby Michael, who is my godson. Marianne Florin, a young woman who teaches photography with Dennis, and Jeanne Murphy, a woman with whom I work at the Arms. We've become very good friends, we are each other's go-to girls. My mother is there with my stepdad;

they're seated at the head of the table, and I'm sure it's a story my mother told that precipitated that laughter. She overdressed for the occasion in a flouncy turquoise chiffon blouse and white linen slacks and silver sandals, but I have to say she looks absolutely beautiful. There was a time when she appeared for a moment to choke on something, and Early laid his hand on her back, and looked over at her. She nodded, *I'm okay,* and he nodded back, and I thought my father was right to suggest she avail herself once more of the comfort of having someone to watch over her, and of watching over someone in return.

Dennis is out there, too, of course, charming the dickens out of everyone.

In the drawer, I find some matches. They're from Fabulous Fern's, a restaurant Penny and I loved. I put them in my pocket with misplaced tenderness.

I used to talk to Penny about a certain kind of discontent I was having in my work. I believed I was doing exactly what I wanted; yet there was something missing, there was always something missing. On a hot day in the last summer we had together, we sat on my porch drinking lemonade, the box of fortunes open, the contents spread out all over the table. I was searching for something I couldn't name, and on this day everything that I consulted offered me exactly nothing.

"Well, look," Penny said. "Maybe your message is off point. What is it that you really want to say? What are you just dying to tell other people? It has to be honest in order for it to really work. It has to be *urgent.*"

I shrugged. I had no answer.

Now I look again at the people gathered in my backyard, feeling a deep appreciation for the events that brought us all together. We are a convergence of fates, a tapestry of fortunes in colors both somber and bright, each contributing equally to the Whole.

I see how the corner of the Compass quilt lifts in the breeze and resettles itself. How, beneath the long table, you can see Riley sleeping. How people have slipped their shoes off, the better to feel the grass between their toes. How baby Michael, his blue eyes wide, has used his palm to plaster banana in the general vicinity of his mouth. How the blush of the peaches looks against the green of the bowl and how the blackened red peppers laid out on a white oval platter glisten with oil. How the tree branches filter light into an unduplicatable pattern. How a solitary lightning bug has appeared to illuminate the base of a bellflower. How plates have been emptied and filled, emptied again and filled again, and how there is still more.

This is what I want to say. This is what I want to tell. But there are no words for it. There is just the tightening of hands, the spread of an odd pressure across the chest. There is just hope.

And faith.

And love.

"Cece?" Dennis calls.

"See you," I tell her.

I go out.

TAPESTRY OF FORTUNES

ELIZABETH BERG

A READER'S GUIDE

THE "HOLD ON A SECOND" PSYCHIC BY ELIZABETH BERG

When I wrote Tapestry of Fortunes, *I knew I wanted to include aspects of divination. It was for whimsical as well as more serious reasons. I wouldn't say I believe entirely in the prognostic statements of Runes or Tarot cards or people who call themselves psychics, but there can be times when readings are eerily dead on. One of the first times I went to a psychic, I had a lot of fun with a pretty eccentric character. But there was something about the experience that let me know there was more to the business of inquiring of the oracle than I had thought. Here's what happened.*

Claire Brightwater is the proprietor of Earth Dancer Gallery. This is a shop situated over a shoe store and next to a weight loss clinic. You can buy all kinds of Native American things there: kachina dolls, beautiful stones, feathers, books and tapes, blankets and jewelry and medicine wheels. Also, you can take advantage of Claire's psychic abilities. You know she has them because of the sign in her window. PSYCHIC, it says.

So I make an appointment for a reading. And when I arrive, I'm a little late and apologetic and out of breath. "Sorry," I say. "Sorry."

She holds up her bracelet-laden arm. "No problem." She pulls a chair up next to her desk. "Here," she says. "Sit down. Center your-self." She has long, flaming-red hair. She is wearing a purple shawl and a colorful, long skirt and many rings. She is a wonder to behold, one of those women who look so good overweight that you want to be overweight, too. I put my jacket and purse on the floor and she says, "No, you have to get *centered*," and puts my purse under me and my jacket behind me. "There," she says. "Now, I'll just pay some bills here while you hold some crystals." She puts a pink one in my right hand and a purple one in my left. While she makes out checks, I hold the crystals tight. I see another homemade sign against one of the counters. NO PLASTIC. CHECKS OKAY. BARTERING OKAY. In a little while, she looks up. "Okay?" I nod. She checks the pink crystal. "This is for love," she says. "Your heart is *full* of love." She nods, agreeing with herself. "Yes. Very beautiful." Then she takes the purple crystal. "This is for stress," she says. "This is cold. You got a lot of stress." Now I nod, thinking, *Well, I'm alive on the earth. Why wouldn't I have stress?* Claire's advice to me about stress is this: "You need to go back to the earth. You need to lie down on it, first on your back, arms and legs spread out. Then lie on your front, and listen to the pulse of the earth." This sounds like fine advice to me. I used to do it all the time when I was a kid. And I had much less stress then, come to think of it.

She tells me she sees a lot of oscillating around me. "You're going back and forth, back and forth inside, aren't you?" We stare intently at each other. The phone rings. "Excuse me," she says. Then, into the phone, "Hello, Earth Dancer Gallery." I'm thinking, wait a minute. What kind of reading is this? But she takes care of the call and is back to me. She tells me to pull an I Ching card, and I get "Retreat." That sounds good, I tell her. Yes. I definitely need a vacation. Claire suddenly jerks her head up, stares into space. "No . . . note . . .

NOTORIETY!" she says. She looks at me. "This word, it just came to me! Are you trying to be famous or something?"

"Well," I say, "I guess we'd all like to be famous. But I don't know if notoriety is the word I'd pick."

The UPS man comes. Claire tells me to hold on, she'll be right back. She goes over to the counter to pay the man, has a little chat with him. *Sixty dollars I paid for this,* I'm thinking. *Jeez.*

Next we do animal cards. Claire is an all-around kind of psychic. Turns out I'm an owl. "You need to go into the dark for the light," Claire tells me. "That's what this card is saying." Well, I'm all for opposites. You know, the blond beauty, held in the arms of the strong, handsome man, says, "Oh, I hate you, I hate you, I hate you!" just before she kisses him to death. There's something to opposites.

The phone rings again. Claire tells the caller, "He's not here. Can I take a message?" She writes something down, hangs up. "It's time for you to wear a feather in your hair, yes?" she asks me. She picks one out for me. Two dollars.

Now, I know how this is sounding. But the notion of wearing a feather is actually quite appealing. As is lying on the earth. As is a retreat. I'm starting to feel kind of happy. I ask Claire what music is playing in the background. It's very, very soothing. I want it. It's "Lazaris Remembers Lemuria," she tells me. Just so happens I can buy one from her.

"Have you been feeling tired?" Claire asks.

"Yes!" I say. And I really have. Not just I don't want to do the dishes tired. I've been *deep* tired.

She nods. "All the women around here are tired," she says. "It's because of our connection to the earth. The earth is having a very hard time giving birth to spring this year, and we all feel it."

A customer comes in, a woman just looking. "I'm doing a reading,"

Claire says, "but just let me know if you need any help." A few minutes later, there's another phone call, someone wanting to know about the upcoming pipe ceremony. Claire tells them all about it.

"Your work, you need to pay attention to what comes from the heart." She looks at me, shakes her head. "You will have great success."

Another customer, a teenage boy wearing a T-shirt featuring crystals, looking for bumper stickers. No bumper stickers. But Claire sells him some little rocks.

We finish up and I realize I am feeling calmer and more centered than I have in a long time. Some of what Claire said felt silly. And some of it felt scary-true. Whatever has happened, I feel better than I ever have after any therapy session. Plus I got a feather and a tape and permission to lie down on the earth.

I guess what I believe is that there is much to the unconscious that we can learn from and be guided by. Is using some tool for fortune telling one of them? Maybe you should find out for yourself. If you're not enlightened, you'll at least be entertained. That's my prediction.

1. Cecelia is a motivational speaker who preaches that "getting lost is the only way to find what you didn't know you were looking for" (8). Do you think Cecelia is able to take her own advice? How does moving in with Lise, Joni, and Renie help her explore this philosophy?

2. Throughout the novel, Cecelia and the other women often rely on her box of fortunes to help them search for answers to their big questions. How do these answers affect their decision-making? Do their fortunes make a difference, or is it something else that ultimately guides them to these answers?

3. "I, the motivational speaker, have not been able to motivate myself into making a new life without her," Cecelia says, referring to Penny's death (10). What eventually changes for Cecelia and enables her to start a new life? Does Penny play a part in this change, even after her death?

4. When Brice, Penny's husband, tells Cece that he is getting re-married, she is initially surprised, but also happy that he is moving

on. "People with people, good. People alone, bad," Penny always used to say to Cece (35). Is it difficult for Cece to heed this advice? Why might it be easier for Brice?

5. Soon after Cece receives the postcard from Dennis, she decides to go visit him. What makes Cece so certain about seeing him again? Do you ever get over your first love? How might this relate to Lise's situation?

6. When Cece moves into the house, Renie is initially defensive and skeptical. Her career as a columnist, too, highlights her skeptical and sarcastic tendencies. Why do you think Renie shows only this side of herself for much of the novel? How are the other women eventually able to uncover the more sensitive side of Renie?

7. When Cece volunteers at the Arms and meets Michael, she opens up to him about Penny's death. She explains that it was "one of the most beautiful experiences" of her life (124). What does Cece mean about Penny's death being beautiful? How does that beauty continue to influence Cece's life?

8. Renie asks the women whether they believe in the truth of the saying "Be kind, for everyone is carrying a heavy burden" (174). Wanda, the waitress they meet during the road trip, asserts that although not everyone carries a heavy burden, everyone does carry the burden of fear (175). How is this "burden of fear" a theme throughout the novel?

9. Mother-daughter relationships are central to the story: Renie struggles with meeting her estranged daughter; Lise's daughter urges

her not to reunite with her ex-husband after their divorce; Cece grows annoyed with her mother for acting more like a girlfriend than a parent (110). What makes a mother-daughter relationship so special? What makes it so fraught, and sometimes difficult?

10. After Michael dies, Cece remembers a conversation that she and Penny once had: Cece asked, "What's the point in loving anything when it will just change or be taken away?," and Penny replied, "The point in loving is only that. And when you lose something, you have to remember that then there is room for the next thing. And there is always a next thing." (213) How does this idea relate to the broader theme of the novel? What is the "next thing" that Cece, Phoebe, and the other characters manage to find?

11. Toward the end of the novel, Cece mentions something that Dennis said about photography, which she feels reverberates in her own life: "The greatest understanding of a thing is when you can't reduce it any further." (217) How does this statement relate to Cece's views on love and friendship? How might it relate to your own?

12. Lise, Joni, Renie, and Cecelia are all very different. What do you think makes their relationships with one another thrive, in spite of their differences? Consider how this relates to the quote at the end of the novel: "We are a convergence of fates, a tapestry of fortunes in colors both somber and bright, each contributing equally to the Whole." (218–19)

PHOTO © CURT RICHTER

ELIZABETH BERG is the author of many bestselling novels, including *The Last Time I Saw You, Home Safe, The Year of Pleasures,* and *Dream When You're Feeling Blue,* as well as two collections of short stories and two works of nonfiction. *Open House* was an Oprah's Book Club selection, *Durable Goods* and *Joy School* were selected as ALA Best Books of the Year, *Talk Before Sleep* was short-listed for an Abby Award, and *The Pull of the Moon* was adapted into a play. Berg has been honored by both the Boston Public Library and the Chicago Public Library and is a popular speaker at venues around the country. Her work has been translated into twenty-seven languages. She divides her time between San Francisco and Chicago.